HONI

PAUL BUCK was [...] Escaping from con[...] he became involve[...] working in Better Books and Indica during the week, and by night and at week-ends at UFO, a club where Pink Floyd, Jimi Hendrix and Soft Machine used to play. His first book was *Pimot* (1968), a tale of aborted love. Whilst he has continued writing poetry since that date, publishing over 30 books, including *Lust* (1976), *Violations* (1980), *Ulli's Room* (1981), *Turkish Delight* (1982), *When We Touch* (1985) and *Naming Names* (1988), he also developed his interest in matters of crime. *The Honeymoon Killers* (1970) started as a novelisation of a film, but research into the real-life murderers evolved the book into a more curious novel, gaining early attention in its *Serie Noire* French edition. This Blue Murder edition has been completely revised and reset.

The film quickly became a cult movie and was nominated as the film of the year by critics worldwide. Francoise Truffaut and Michelangelo Antonioni amongst others have rated it as one of their favourite films of all time.

During the 70s, Paul Buck wrote many articles on crime and particularly on psychopaths for an encyclopedia of criminology. At the same time, he was researching his interest in sexuality through the works of French writer Georges Bataille. He edited and published the seminal magazine of the decade *Curtains*, featuring Bataille and many others. In recent times he has directed his interest once again to the exploration of violence and sexuality through his writing.

He has completed two novels, *Bottle* and *Red Ascends* and published his first tough short story 'Back Door Man' in *New Crimes 1*. He is also completing full-length essays on noir writers Jonathan Latimer and Day Keene. In addition, he has translated the lyrics of Jacques Brel for an album by well-known, controversial singer Marc Almond, while penning original lyrics for upcoming singer Melinda Miel.

Series editor: Maxim Jakubowski

Maxim Jakubowski was born in the UK but educated in France. His first book was published when he was only 19. For many years he juggled his writing with an executive position in the food industry before finally switching to book publishing. He has held senior editorial positions with various British publishing houses. An expert on and lover of science fiction, fantasy and crime fiction, he is also known for his books on film and rock music. Among his over twenty books are *Travelling Towards Epsilon, Twenty Houses of the Zodiac, Lands of Never, Beyond Lands of Never, The Complete Book of SF and Fantasy Lists* (with Malcolm Edwards), *The Rock Yearbook*, two volumes of *The Rock Album, The Great Movies—Live* (with Ron van der Meer) and *The Wit and Wisdom of Rock 'n Roll*. He has contributed to many definitive reference works and has edited two leading crime fiction cult imprints: *Black Box Thrillers* and *Blue Murder*. He lives in London.

THE
HONEYMOON KILLERS

PAUL BUCK

Xanadu

blue murder

to Glenda

Thanks to my brother, Peter, for turning me on to the word processor (finally), and for the facilities and help needed in the preparation of this present edition, using Apple® Macintosh™ IIcx and Microsoft® Word.

British Library Cataloguing in Publication Data

Buck, Paul 1946—
  The honeymoon killers.
  I. Title
  823.914 [F]
  ISBN 1-85480-038-8

This revised edition published 1990 in the Blue Murder series by Xanadu Publications Limited, 19 Cornwall Road, London N4 4PH.

Printed and bound in Great Britain by
Cox & Wyman Limited, Reading.

THE INCREDIBLE SHOCKING DRAMA
YOU ARE ABOUT TO READ IS PERHAPS THE
MOST BIZARRE EPISODE IN THE ANNALS
OF AMERICAN CRIME.
THE UNBELIEVABLE EVENTS DEPICTED
ARE BASED ON NEWSPAPER ACCOUNTS
AND COURT RECORDS.
THIS IS A TRUE STORY.

MARTHA BECK AND RAYMOND
FERNANDEZ WERE ELECTROCUTED IN
SING SING PRISON ON MARCH 8, 1951.

MARTHA

Boom!

Clouds of white smoke billowed from around a laboratory door.

Martha appeared from her office and marched down the corridor to the scene.

"What happened?" she demanded instantly.

Through the clearing smoke she discerned a coughing Severns...and Jackson.

Standing on the antiquated radiator, attempting to wrench down a window, Jackson replied:

"Someone made a little mistake and let some chlorine and ammonia get together. I don't think she'll do it again."

Martha took an immediate dislike to his mocking tone and turned to face the still coughing nurse.

"You again, Severns. Are you all right?"

"I think so, Miss Beck. I didn't realize it was ammonia."

The orderly's strains were rewarded -- the window squeaked open.

"Good thing I was here," he said. "She could have been hurt."

Martha was catching on. She moved firmly towards the young man to confront him. She stood solid, her fists clenched at her side.

"What were you doing in here, Jackson? Why aren't you in the ward where you belong?"

Jackson turned to face the Moby Dick, as he was apt to regard her, and resumed his mocking manner -- folding his arms and leaning back against the window.

"Oh, *now* I see what happened," said Martha. And raising her voice, she bellowed: "I don't give a damn what you do outside this hospital. But here, you're as bad as the ammonia and chlorine. Now get out of here, Jackson!"

He did not intend to show his fear of this huge mammal with the broad and bowed forehead. How could anyone fall for that?

With a courageous shrug, he jumped down, casually.

"This is a hospital laboratory, not a motel room," Martha said sternly. Her eyes hardened. "I don't want to see you in here again. Do you understand me?"

"I think so, Miss Beck," he replied as he strolled from the room, glancing at Severns with a grin spread across his face like thick clotted cream.

Martha followed to hurry him out. She turned to the two nurses who now stood in the doorway.

"Everything's all right. Go back to your stations."

Her voice was calm. The mark of a well-trained nurse. Adaptability to the situation. No unnecessary display of emotions to disturb others.

They shunted off.

She turned back and resumed her disciplinary role.

"As for you, Severns, I'll deal with you later. You've already kept me overtime. I want you in my office first thing tomorrow morning."

Cowering in the corner, the nurse squeaked as much as the window had done. But her sounds formed words.

"I'm sorry, Miss Beck."

"You'll be a lot sorrier if you're ever out of line with me again."

Martha emerged from the old training laboratory and hurried back to her office where she prepared to leave the hospital.

Such slight disturbances were not uncommon. Nevertheless they were tiresome and a threat to her employment. She was a good nurse. Competent. Neat. She had earned her position as Supervisor of Nurses. Having worked in other hospitals, and despite numerous other unjust rejections, she was now firmly ensconced. She would die, thrown out of the ocean. All the girls liked her, for she was kind-hearted and understanding, although she could be firm when required. Her high level of intelligence helped her to be efficient and effective. Minor events were irritating, for if the authorities wished to dismiss her they would turn them into major events to suit the purpose -- as they had done previously when she had hung around bus depots talking to the drivers.

Martha would not tolerate incidents. She was resigned to devoting all her energies to her work, for her personal life -- more precisely, her lovelife -- was a failure. It had been so ever since she grew fat in her youth. At first she became bitter, as her name suggested.* But when she was aware that she would be unable to have her dream-boy, she gave all she had to the hospital and humanity. It had been said that she would go far in her vocation. But they had omitted to stipulate their intended meaning of "far". Her many positions had led her to the West Coast...and back.

With these thoughts she let her hair down and pulled on a beige mackintosh.

Tired, she propelled herself towards the bus stop.

As she trudged along the sidewalk she reflected upon Jackson's contemptuous manner. If she couldn't have amours at work, neither could they. Only once had a doctor made a pass at her, and that was when she worked in a mortuary. He was old and past it anyway. No orderly had ever made advances. Nor even a porter. In fact, no one in her profession. The only man who had paid her any amative attention in a hospital was Joe. He had been a patient in California, the land of one's dreams. Although she wouldn't admit it, she was jealous of her girls being eyed and seduced under her very nose. Particularly when the seducer was a half-wop. She would have to report him to his superiors. The

---

* **Martha** (Heb.), becoming bitter.

sooner he was fished out the better.

She kicked a child's wagon out of her path, as she would kick Jackson out of her see at Mobile City Hospital.

Martha entered her home, a pleasant (if untidy) apartment in the suburbs. She had taken the place with her mother after returning from the West Coast three years before. Life with Momma was better than being alone even though it was a strain on her energy. Martha badly needed the security her company provided, and which the hospital never entirely assured her.

The apartment was not huge, though neither was Martha's wage. But it was comfortable enough for two. And the decor was pleasant.

Bunny, her neighbor, was sprawled on the couch reading one of Martha's confession magazines.

She jumped up with a sigh of relief when Martha stumbled in laden with a bag of groceries.

"Hi, Hon," she said, eyeing the bag.

Martha slumped into a chair by the table.

"Oh, Jesus. I feel like I've swum the Gulf."

She was all in. She looked a mess, her coat bursting apart as if wrapped round a sack of potatoes. Outside work her appearance was becoming more slovenly. Left a lot to be desired would be the wrong thing to say, for the 230 pounds of blubber and pendulous breasts did nothing for the style of her clothes. And, of course, the heat didn't help any.

"Hot, huh?' Bunny commented, noticing Martha's sweaty features. "And it's only April. I hope you got some beer in there. We're out."

Bunny took the groceries from her and moved towards the kitchen.

"D'ya remember last April. It was a real heatwave. Louis was staying then..." She droned on.

Where was Momma?

"I thought you were gonna keep her company?"

10

"Who?"

"Momma," said Martha, irritably, wiping a hand under her chins.

"Well, she said she wanted to lie down," Bunny lied, "so I said 'why don't you go into my bedroom and lie down till Martha comes home then I can do my housework.'" She returned, still chattering. "But no, no, she had to lie down in her *own* bed. I'm telling you she's the Queen Mother."

She flapped her hands regally and laughed.

Martha was too weary for cat-&-mouse games. No matter how big the cats were, or the mice, come to that. She admitted defeat. Not only to Bunny's ears, but also to Momma who had awoken at the sound of the front door.

"Now, she can't help it if she's senile. Oh gee I'm all in." And she heaved a sigh of exhaustion.

Bunny took the hint.

"Okay, listen. Let me give you your mail before I forget it and walk off with it."

Collecting the mail from the side, she brought it to Martha, and then headed back to the kitchen, muttering: "Boy, is she a pain in the ass."

Bills and advertisements. Martha flipped through the envelopes, not bothering to open the usuals. One, however, held her attention.

It was a plain, cheap envelope with no indication of its sender.

She slit it with her fingernail and extracted a badly printed pamphlet.

AUNT CARRIE'S FRIENDSHIP CLUB
523 Green Street
Los Angeles, California

And further down:

Her heart sunk.

Her throat went dry.

She gulped bitterly.

Memories and thoughts whirlpooled.

What bastard sent this? Tommy. Tommy again. He joked poked about it. The bar. Last week. Torments me so. They all taunt me, oh. Why? I. All of them. Always. Always will. Well, it's not funny. No, Tommy, no. Nor that slimming thing you sent. Thought it funny. Twisted. Fuck you. I hate you, I hate you. How I hate you. I do. Fat. Too fat. Now I'm too fat. Just cos I'm fat. Forget it. Never. Never ever leave me alone. Why can't they? Hurts. How it hurts. Go on. I can't. The end. Dead. Wish I was dead, I do, I do, I do. This time I do, I do, I do. Dead. I do...

Dry tears flowed through her body, and her skin wept.

Heartbroken, she stamped her clammy body into the kitchen.

"Look at this!" Martha exclaimed disgustedly. "Who sent this? I never applied for anything like this."

She sank into a chair and despair.

From inside the refrigerator rose Bunny's voice.

"What's the matter with it?"

"What is it, some kind of April Fool's Day joke? If it is it stinks!"

Martha turned to the table and seized upon a packet of pretzels with which to swallow her pride and stifle her tears.

Bunny knew about the letter, but did not recognize the seriousness of the crime in Martha's mind.

"I thought you were going on a diet?" was all she said "What are you eating the pretzels for now? You're gonna have supper soon. They're full of salt, then you start drinking like a fish. You know how fattening that is."

"Leave me alone, won't ya," Martha cried, forced almost to the verge of tears. Not even her best friend understood.

Always talking, never thinking. "D'ya mind?" She flung the packet to the floor.

From the ice-box came Bunny. She *had* offended Martha. Christ, she hadn't meant to.

"Would I have sent in your name if I knew it would upset you like this?"

Martha could not believe it.

"You sent it?" Martha croaked incredulously.

Why? But why?

By now Mrs.Beck had heard the explosion and had come to investigate. But not with the same firmness as Martha had earlier. This investigation was irritation.

"Martha. What's the matter with my little girl?"

"Stop it, Momma. I'm not your little girl?"

When one's daughter says such things and looks so distressed, it has only one meaning.

"It isn't some *man* you're mixed up with, is it?"

"Don't, Momma. Please!"

Bunny intervened. That was the worst possible thing Mrs.Beck could have said. Especially now.

"Oh why don't you leave your daughter alone? Can't you see how upset she is?"

Mrs.Beck needed to reinstate herself upon the throne. She ruled here, not this upstart.

"She's been mean to me *all* day long," she accused. "Now I'm going to lie down in my *own* bed."

She expected sympathy, and Martha obliged, as always.

"That's a good idea, Momma. I'll call you when supper's ready."

She knew how to handle Momma, how to avoid further commotion.

Her mother having carried her frail body back to the bedroom, Martha turned passively on her friend.

"Thanks for the April Fool's Day joke."

"Aw, come on, Martha. For Chrissake, what kind of a friend do you think I am? Sure I sent in your name."

"What ya do it for?"

"You just look at this."

Bunny reached for one of the many romance magazines strewn about the apartment and leafed through to the relevant advertisement. She pointed to the photograph and then read beneath:

NO MORE LONELY NIGHTS FOR THESE TWO LUCKY PEOPLE

BUT WAS IT REALLY LUCK?

No, it was Aunt Carrie who brought them together. She has helped hundreds of women to find suitable mates, carefully selected from her long list of lonely but eligible men who are seekingeven as you are seekingto find true happiness in a blissful marriage. Many of the men on her list are gay, witty, charming, and have good positions or are independently wealthy. Why should you not meet such men? Aunt Carrie can open

the door to exciting new friendships for you. Why not drop her a line? It may change your lonely life.

Martha did not seem quite convinced by the sentimental clichés read out to her. She needed pushing. Bunny could tell.

"Martha, you just *need* a man. Oh listen, you're a little on the heavy side, but you're not an old hag you know. You could be pretty sexy with the right man."

And more:

"Come on. Let's fill it out. What have you got to lose?"

Joe. I've got Joe, Martha thought. He's mine alone. But she could not answer aloud.

"Here, before you change your mind. Come on now. I'll help you with it. Where's the pen?"

"In the cabinet. You sure this is all right?"

"What have you got to lose?"

The pen was placed in Martha's hand. Martha obeyed her. She was too tired to object further.

"All these questions. Do I *have* to tell the truth?"

"So who's puttin' you on the witness stand?"

"I suppose there's no harm in it. Do you think someone will really write to me?"

"There's only one way to find out and someday you might even thank me for it."

The task was begun. Martha completed the form, distorting a few facts to make herself more appealing. Then, taking out some special pink stationary (a birthday present), she wrote a letter stating the type of man she wanted. He was right out of a romance magazine. Tall. Dark. Handsome. A match for Joe. Enclosing a five-dollar bill, she sealed the envelope and in her small, neat, businesslike handwriting wrote the address. She reflected proudly on the style that had

15

won her a prize at school.

As she walked to the mailbox later that evening, she wondered what sort of reply she would receive. Would it be some nice man? Suppose it was an old man, or a funny sort? What then? She felt sure she would be able to cope with the situation. She was pretty tough. Besides, why should she be less fortunate than anyone else? She bet some of the women were real old bags! But it said they all got husbands. Suppose hers was quite handsome? The joke would be on everyone: Bunny, Momma, all at the bar, and at the hospital.

She felt less grouchy and depressed now. She even discovered enough energy to continue down the block and buy a box of candy and another magazine.

*

Martha's hopes might have been raised higher had she known that April 1st was the festival of Venus. And that April was the month of beauty and sensual love for the goddess.

RAY

The Lonely Heart was forwarded to Raymond Fernandez on a list of recent recruitments.

There was no discrimination between male members. Big or small, they all received the list. The letters were merely to encourage the women who wrote them, and bore no weight. Except in Martha's case, where by coincidence, Ray resembled her desired description.

He plumped for her with his magic pin and commenced the correspondence.

Dear Martha,

I hope you'll allow me the liberty of addressing you by your Christian name. To tell the truth I don't quite know how to begin this letter to you because, I must confess, this is the first letter of this sort I have ever written.

Would you like to know a little about me? I'm thirty-four and I've been told I'm not a bad looking fellow. I am in the importing business from Spain my mother country. I live alone here in this apartment much too large for a bachelor but I hope someday to share it with a wife.

Why did I choose you for my debut friendship letter? Because you are a nurse and therefore I know you have a full heart with a great capacity for comfort and love.

Your friend,
Raymond Fernandez

He sat back and smiled at his handiwork. He had acquired the art of writing alluring letters through much practice. All the phrases that women loved to hear and read would be incorporated into the forthcoming series. It was becoming quite a regular routine.

Venus's flytrap reopened.

Scattered about his writing table were many photographs of the victims which *Dionaea muscipula* had caught: blondes, brunettes, ugly, fat, thin, deformed. Most were middle-aged. Martha was twenty-seven, one of the few younger de Milo's. That did not matter. Martha was not the exotic name he would have preferred. That did not matter. She held a good position, and no doubt a good income. *That* did matter. He had to make a living since he had not held down a steady job -- not since the accident.

The letter thrilled Martha. It had arrived as she left for work. Throughout the day she took it out again and again, read and re-read it. To Martha, whose love was confession magazines, this letter conveyed sincerity. Raymond sounded so nice. Like Joe.

On the way home that night she bought some expensive stationary -- with roses on the letterhead.

She wrote to him.

He wrote back.

Letters went to and fro.

Ray sent a photograph of himself.

Martha was knocked out. The joke *was* on everyone. He looked something like Charles Boyer.

She returned a photograph of herself, amongst a group of six nurses. She was well hidden at the back. For good measure she wrote:

It doesn't do me justice.

She prayed her size would not stand out.

It did not. Ray had trapped so many shapes and sizes that she seemed no more unusual than the others. Just another to

18

be fleeced.

When he had joined the club two years back, not long after the accident, he had written and met women for amatory purposes. None had been suitable partners for marriage. Had he found one, he would not have hesitated, even though he had a wife in Spain. When one woman gave him money as a gift, it occurred to him that he could make monetary gains from others. From then on, his contacts had been engaged primarily as a source of income. His larcenies, although petty, required him to obtain a postal box number in case of prospective major strikes. More often he corresponded from his apartment. Out of a few dozen affairs he reckoned only one would sue for robbery. The others would pass it off as expenses -- a fair compensation for the few days of happiness and affection his charm afforded them whilst the romance blossomed and was professionally plucked.

The exchange grew more intimate.

He thought the moment to move was ripening. He asked for a lock of Martha's hair.

She sent it.

With the hair he could perform the ritual of hypnotism, which he had adapted from the Voodoo rites he had learnt in prison.

It had happened whilst he was serving a short spell for a minor stealing offense, shortly after the accident. His fellow inmates were mainly West Indians. They had intrigued him with tales of the power of Voodoo, particularly the power one could hold over another by hypnotism. He felt sure that his first effort, which had been to secure an early release, had succeeded solely through his concentrating upon the judge. On his release he had bought William Seabrook's **Magic Island** and had spent long periods studying it. With the discovery of his unlimited power he had set out to charm the opposite sex.

The lock of Martha's hair he placed within his locket. Filling the room with the fumes of incense, he willed

Martha to love him.

The time had come. The plant was about to spring. He intended to visit her. He announced his arrival by letter and quickly followed it with a telegram.

At the eleventh hour Martha became afraid. The little discrepancies between fact and fiction, which had seemed so harmless, suddenly loomed out of all proportion. Would the charming Don Quixote reject her on sight? Too many gallant gentlemen had.

In spite of the odds, she carried on with the preparations.

She arranged a few days leave from the hospital.

She spring-cleaned the apartment.

She stocked the refrigerator.

The day arrived.

The sun was shining.

A warm wind breezed in from the Gulf.

Momma was made to wear her best white dress,

Martha dressed with extra care. She was determined to outdo herself. She would outstrip Circe.

It sprung.

On arrival Ray was stunned beyond measure by Martha's appearance. He had not expected such a large woman. Her photograph had not prepared him for such an ordeal. But he did not reveal his feelings. She oozed personality and offered hospitality. He accepted and was led to the smooth stone home of the enchantress.

Martha was terribly excited. He was exactly as she had imagined him to be. He did not look *something* like Charles Boyer, he was *just* like Charles Boyer. In manner as well as appearance.

Charles Boyer was her Hollywood hero. She had seen every one of his pictures that had come to the local theater:

The Garden of Allah, with Marlene Dietrich
History is Made at Night
Conquest, with Greta Garbo
Love Affair, with Irene Dunne
When Tomorrow Comes, with Irene Dunne
Tales of Manhattan, with Rita Hayworth and
    Ginger Rogers
The Constant Nymph, with Joan Fontaine
Gaslight, with Ingrid Bergman
Confidential Agent, with Lauren Bacall
Cluny Brown, with Jennifer Jones

She also had an autographed photograph. At first it had
been stood on the bureau, but later had been reduced to a
home in a drawer when a friend pulled her leg over the star.

Dapper, in his all-white suit, his big striped tie, and with
his Panama on his head, Ray looked the perfect Don Juan.

She wore a black dress to look slimmer.

After the three of them had dined, Martha produced more
wine.

The potion.

Ray was relaxing in an armchair having thoroughly
enjoyed the meal. He paid the routine compliment.

"Oh, I can't move. That was a wonderful dinner."

"I made the pecan pie," Mrs.Beck said, trying to reclaim
the limelight.

"Oh, the very best part of the meal, Mrs.Beck,"
complimented Ray again.

Mrs.Beck was delighted by the unusual praises that
bloomed from his pleasant flowery speech. The more he said,
the more they went to her head.

She giggled.

"Do you want another drink, Momma?"

"Another drink? You don't usually let me have even one."

She *was* being spoilt.

"Well, this is a very special occasion."

Martha poured it and went into the kitchen to fetch another bottle.

"I have a record I want to play for you," giggled Mrs.Beck.

"For me? How kind."

"I'll find it in a minute."

"Thank you," smiled Ray.

He turned his attention back to the other female.

"What about you, Martha?" Ray called. "You haven't even had your first."

"Just a little one then. I'm counting calories," answered Martha. She thought that was a good answer to indicate she was rapidly losing weight. Not that she ever would, so the doctors had told her, but she could always pretend.

Getting up from his armchair, Ray excused himself from Mrs.Beck's presence and crossed towards the kitchen.

"I'll help you get it," he said as he entered.

In one hand Martha held a drink, in the other -- a pill. She looked down at it. He followed her eyes.

Unsure, she said: "Would you think I'm terrible if I gave her this?"

Slowly he raised his head. Their eyes met. His mouth widened to a smile of victory.

"No," he murmured. "I want to be alone, too."

She was held spellbound. Transfixed in his dark, deep-set eyes.

Ray leaned forward and kissed her.

Her heart leapt at the magic touch. He was hers. She would possess him. Would never let him part. Blow Joe, he could go. Ray was here to stay. Her body sang.

When they reappeared, Martha crossed to her mother who was half-asleep on her couch. Martha wanted to be doubly sure, and proffered the pill.

"Take your vitamin pill, Momma."

"I've already had my vitamin pill, this morning," protested

Mrs.Beck weakly.

"No, I forgot to give it to you."

"This one looks different."

"It's a new kind I got at the hospital," Martha said, in her own tactful way.

"How she babies me," Mrs.Beck said to Ray, at Martha's side.

They smiled and she slipped the pill down.

"Did you find your record, Mrs.Beck?" questioned Ray.

"Yes, I did. See, this is the record I found for Ray." She picked it up from beside her. "I want you to play it because I like him. He is the nicest beau you ever had, Martha. Better than Joe." Even she was convinced of the legendary figure. She giggled. "It's the *Latin from Manhattan*."

"Oh, Momma. That's not funny."

Martha glanced at Ray. He was not offended. He looked as charmed as ever. Was he in love with her, like she was in love with him?

She slid the record onto the turntable.

There he goes again, the darling, she thought.

"No, I think it's charming. A record in my honor. Thank you, *bella señora. Besasare tus manos.*" And with that he made a slow graceful bow to Mrs.Beck, kissed her hand, and then swung his tall, well-built body into a dance.

"Who wants to rumba with me?"

I do, thought Martha. But she knew better.

"I do, I do," said Mrs.Beck, drowsily, and flickered out.

"Do it yourself. We'll watch," Martha had to be content to say.

He danced on, fingers snapping high above his head, hips swaying.

¡*Caramba*!

He had now lived in Manhattan for almost a year. His life had been one long Odyssey. Born in Hawaii of Spanish parents, they moved to Connecticut when he was three. In his early youth he returned to Spain, where he married. A

23

frustrated spell of work in his native land and he was off to New York, leaving his wife and child with the promise he would send for them. Almost immediately his son became ill and he journeyed back. Civil War prevented him leaving again on his son's recovery. Then World War II. Finally he set off for the States, promising his wife that he would send for her, so they could divorce in America. It never happened. Instead, the accident.

He stepped his way towards Martha. She was no Venus, but her features were well formed and her cheek bones high. Signs that denoted beauty, shamefully cushioned in fat.

"She's asleep," he said, a twinkle in his eye.

Martha's eyes responded and sparkled as she reached for him from her position on the couch. She put her hands on his waist. He continued to dance between her arms, like a dream.

His fingers tampered with the table lamp, turned it off.

"Let's put her in the bedroom."

"No, she won't bother us," he answered gently. "Here, give me your hand." He guided it towards his flies. And bending his strong Spanish accent, he ventured seductively: "Don't be a *shy* little nurse."

His eyes compelled her through the darkness. He came down upon her, blanketing.

That night Momma's little girl experienced full sexual satisfaction for the first time. Orgasm upon orgasm was laid as the warrior unfolded his vast experience from America to Spain and back again. The lonesome traveler fell into the pit of the goddess. She worked him for her every response. By morning he was wholly frightened and a total wreck. He cursed the powers that had brought about this venue.

Wednesday they spent together. Ray couldn't extricate himself immediately as he had already promised to stay a few days. Besides, he had to remain in bed till lunchtime. Martha insisted. By then it was too late to escape. Ray conceded to the situation and settled back quietly for the rest of the day. The highlight of the afternoon was when Bunny visited. He found her entertaining and amusing, for the limited time that Martha allowed before she ushered her out. Dinner followed and then they retired to bed, to get some sleep as well.

Ray far exceeded the dreams of Martha's romance magazines. His enlistment meant that Joe could be relieved. The handsome Lieutenant Commander was a fabrication of her mind. She had told her friends he was currently at sea. He would now be killed in action. She would burn him from her thoughts. He had met his match.

Thursday morning Ray arose early and decided it was time to leave.

Martha's scenes, professing her love for him and her demands of marriage, scared him. Further, she did not have much money. She seemed to eat it.

He told her of his departure, giving ample reasons for his return to New York.

She broke into tears. She never wanted to let him go. She knew she would never see him again. She had been unable to transform him into an animal to keep. But keep him she must.

She cried, and cried, and cried again.

He tried to comfort her.

"Honey, don't cry again."

"I can't help it. I couldn't think of you going."

Tomorrow she was expected back at work. She did not care. It was unimportant. Ray was determined to leave. With the little money she had given him he could expect to cover his expenses and a bit more. More than that, he would be thankful to have escaped unscathed from this uncontrollable nightmare. Flee rather than fleece was the policy.

He continued to back out, using his charm to find the door handle.

25

"If I'm not home when the dye account comes, I can't see you again." He frowned, searching for words. He could only repeat himself, for no one had been as obstreperous as Martha. "I've lost hundreds of dollars. I couldn't even have had yesterday if it wasn't for your loan. I would have to be back in New York today before the banks close."

Finally and grudgingly she let him depart.

But only after he had promised : eye to eye : that he would return as soon as possible.

He promised -- his accident -- and counted his blessings (and earnings) all the way back to New York.

BUNNY

Each day Martha expected a reply to her daily letters. Each day she awaited the word which would tell her he was coming back, or she should go to him. Each day she expressed the burning love that devoured her.

But there were no replies.

Joe had never let her down.

And then one morning the doorbell dragged her from the throes of a bad dream.

Pulling her robe hastily about her, she opened the door, leaving the chain on its hook.

"What is it?" she inquired.

"Special delivery for Miss Beck."

At last!

Her enthusiasm didn't show as her voice, still slurred from sleep, replied:

"I'm Miss Beck."

She pulled the letter through the gap and shut the door.

She went no further. She leaned back against it, slit open the letter.

A glance revealed its content.

God no! He can't do this to me. I won't allow it.

Her next thought was to summon help.

Turning quickly, she opened the door and ran across the hall to Bunny's apartment.

"Bunny! Bunny! Let me in!" she hammered on the paneling.

The letter was thrust beneath Bunny's nose as she waved past and burst into the bedroom.

Bunny's boyfriend, John, sat up at the intrusion.

Martha ignored him, flung her hulk onto the bed, and

wept.

"What can I do? What can I do?" she sobbed.

Bunny did not comprehend. She withdrew the letter from Martha's grasp and read it through.

"Oh Hon," she sympathized.

"I want to die. I want to die."

"Now now, honey. Don't say that."

Bunny patted Martha's arm whilst she mulled over the problem.

Ideas leapt about her mind. For the last sixteen years, half her life, she had kept her wits about her where love matters were concerned. She had enjoyed her fair share of men for the ten years since her divorce. The alimony was sufficient to keep her modest apartment and her looks in good shape. She retained her attractiveness, her moderate figure and, above all, her energy, of which she possessed a lot. It enabled her to bound into bed with the best of them. John, her latest, was no great shakes, but he knew what she wanted and gave it willingly.

John sank back, divorcing himself from the goddesses meeting on the Mount.

"I have an idea," Bunny said suddenly.

"What?"

"Wait and see."

She picked up the telephone and dialed.

"Hello. Operator. I want you to get me a New York number." And to Martha:"What's his address?"

Ray awoke, turned on the light, and answered.

"Hello...What?...I don't believe it...Were the police there?...Of course you shouldn't call the police."

La policia. That was all he needed. The damn fool.

Cockily he lent his ear to Bunny's tale.

He was flattered. A woman would do that for him? But thank God she did not call the police. That would ruin him.

"Wonderful, Bunny. Can't live without me? Can't I talk to

the poor darling?" he cooed.

Bunny was crouched over the phone, beginning to enjoy herself. Her idea was working. It had come easily to her, for Martha often talked about suicide, and had even gone so far as to try a couple of times.

"Oh, no, she doesn't even know I'm calling. I'm calling from my apartment. Oh, you don't know *how* sick she is from all that gas."

Martha had recovered from her sobs and sat on the edge of the bed, wishing she could speak. Now that she had pulled herself together, John started to toy with her arm.

"We can thank our lucky stars I got to her in time," said Bunny, twitching her nose in the excitement. "What a story for the newspapers...What?"

She had played for his reply. She glanced at Martha. It was working. So was John.

"Oh, get away from her. Leave her alone," she said to him. "Ray, uh, no, that was my new little puppy. He was jumping all over Martha and I was afraid he might wake her up." She had blundered. She rabbited on hastily: "Did I say that? Oh well, I'm just nervous. I don't know what I'm saying...Oh, no. She's here in my apartment. In my bed...Oh, I wouldn't leave her alone. I -- I don't know what she'd do...Oh no, she can't talk to you. She's unconscious."

Martha was dying to talk to Ray, but Bunny held her off with her hand. Martha had to say something. Do something. She perched on the edge of the bed and produced a suitably faked moan.

"Ray, Ray, I wanna say hi. I wanna say hi," she added.

Bunny turned to Martha. She was thoroughly enjoying the circus. She felt like laughing at her own act. Being the ring master she had to play it straight. She held the whip hand.

"Martha, Martha," she called in a ghostly tone. "It's me, Bunny. Ray's on the phone."

Both had temporarily forgotten John, who was lying in the background wracked with laughter.

Martha made a grab for the phone. Bunny pulled away, clowning. She had got Ray in the first place. Now she was the fulcrum. Without her, things would fall flat.

"She won't come to the phone. She says you don't love her and she wants to die." She paused. "She says you'll read about it in the papers when she kills herself." She paused again and prayed for his reply. It came. "Wait a minute, Ray."

She signaled Martha to come to the phone. Covering the mouthpiece, she whispered juicily:

"He says he *loves* you."

Overjoyed at the fact, Martha smiled. His wretched letter had meant nothing.

"Ray, I think she'll come to the phone now."

Bunny teased Martha, holding the wire high out of reach. Martha begged her way into the arena before she was presented with the receiver.

The path paved, Bunny sat back on her haunches, shaking her light-brown waves at her achievement.

"Hello, Ray."

"Darling, I didn't mean it," he sugared.

"Ray, listen. You gotta come down here. If you don't I'll - - I'll kill myself, I swear."

"Oh, I can't get away now, sweetheart...Would you like to come up *here* for a little visit?"

That settled it. She packed immediately and arranged for a two-week leave of absence.

Ray too was determined to settle this once and for all. Any doubts of Martha's sincerity would be cleared up. Initially he did not think she would come, but when, to his surprise, she arrived, he told her everything: his source of income; his large sexual appetite; his Voodoo beliefs; his inability to remain with one woman in one place; the five f's and his sixth -- find 'em, feel 'em, finger 'em, fuck 'em, *fleece 'em*, forget 'em. All this he thought would send her packing.

But Martha was adamant. She had set herself on him, and she meant to have him. Even if it required the complete debasement and humiliation of herself. She frankly declared her dislike of his line of business, but agreed to help. She would do anything to be with him and please him, as she had done previously for her mother. His love was omnipotent. Her love was obsessive.

She did not even mind living in an apartment that he had swindled from a previous victim, who had subsequently died whilst on holiday.

Ray could not believe it. This had *never* happened before. Not that he often had so much trouble in disposing of the occasional vine. Pride prevailed at an earlier stage.

He persisted with his interrogation.

"Now that you know everything about me, do you still love me?"

"Yes."

"Will you still commit suicide for me?"

"Yes."

"You don't want to call the police? You don't want to sue me?"

She turned and looked into his powerful eyes.

"No."

His tension was relieved with a loud sigh. He shrugged his shoulders in resignation.

Esta loca. The crazy little fool.

He was stuck with her. He supposed she *could*, if necessary, be his partner in crime.

After all, he had very little choice, considering the alternatives.

During the following two weeks Martha ran around doing his daily chores, and his nightly ones. Each time it was better for her. Ray was satisfied too, even though she was not the ideal Venus to maneuver around the bed.

"Can we get married soon?" she asked one night towards

the end of her stay, as they lay relaxing in bed.

"I have to go through with this senseless marriage to the Acker woman," he reminded. "I can't get out of it. Wait until after that. You've got to go back to Mobile anyway. Couldn't leave your mother with that woman forever. Go back to the hospital."

"How can I, knowing you're with another woman?"

"I won't touch her. I promise. I'll get everything from her before the wedding," he emphasized.

"There'll be no honeymoon?"

"Dump her right away. I don't want it to last a second longer than necessary. It's not like this."

"Then you'll come back to Mobile?"

"Yes. We'll work our future out together. I promise."

This time his promise was truthful, his words were sincere. His eyes told her so.

Her cunning had trapped the seaman.

To seal the promise Martha kissed the St.Christopher locket that lay on his hairy chest.

MOMMA

When Martha returned to the hospital she was faced by a different scene from that she had expected. One of the directors accompanied her to her office and took up a position behind her desk.

"After Mrs.Flynn called," he started, "to say you'd gone to New York, I came in here to find the assignment chart. I'm afraid you left some of your rather torrid correspondence with a Mr.Fernandez in New York." He pronounced the name with a slow nasal accent and opened the folder. "I think you'd better take it with you. I don't think our board of directors would look kindly on our Supervisor of Nurses being involved in a lonely hearts scandal."

The folder was thrown on the desk between them.

Martha was flabbergasted. How dare the thieving Jew touch her personal things.

She hauled up the drawbridge, and, articulating every syllable, said angrily:

"How dare you go through my desk. You ought to be ashamed of yourself." Hatred flared in her eyes. "I'm not so sure Hitler wasn't right about you people."

"Miss Beck, get out of here before I forget I'm a gentleman."

"You bet I'm getting out of here."

Clutching the letters to her chest, she turned to the door. Reinforcements had to be added to the battlements.

"And don't make the check out to Martha Beck. Make it out to Mrs.Raymond Fernandez," she informed him. "What do you think I am? I went to New York to be married."

With all her reserves brought into force she glanced round at what had been her keep, and stormed off.

She had tried to save her face.

Why was she always hounded? Always rejected? Persecuted? She could have cried.

Despite the hurt she felt, the bright side fired through. The final decision had been made *for* her.

She told Momma and Bunny that she had just quit her job and had already married Ray. Now all she had to do was tell her spouse the good news.

He was not overjoyed at her dismissal -- though wary of the circumstances that surrounded it -- but he was not surprised either. Nor at her announcement that she *had* to return to New York, in spite of her evasion as to the precise reason why.

"I don't mind. Two can live as cheaply as one, darling," she pressed, wallowing snugly and smugly in her chair.

Bunny hopped over and took the phone.

"Let me congratulate the groom. Hi, this is Bunny, Ray...Whadda ya mean 'still the best friend a girl ever had'?...Yeah, now listen. Now that you two have been, uh, spliced...spliced -- married, Ray. Oh now don't you be a stranger, hear?...Oh. Here she is."

She scuttled back to her burrow.

What the hell was happening down there? What story was Martha telling everyone?

"You told her we were *married*?"

"Uh-huh. Momma too," Martha said, taking a bar of candy from her housecoat pocket.

"Jesus, Martha. I go to New Jersey next week to marry Doris Acker. How'm I going to bring her back if you're here? It's impossible. You know I've got to continue my business."

"Don't worry. I'll think of something," she said, chewing over his statement.

Momma entered the lounge, wailing loudly .

"Now what's the matter?"

"Oh, that's Momma. She doesn't want to go to New York."

"Martha! That's completely out of the question. I mean it. Look, you say you love me. Okay. That you're going to kill yourself if you can't come up here. Okay. *But you can't bring the old lady.*"

"What else am I gonna do with her?"

"Get rid of her. Choke her. I don't care what the hell you do with her. But you can't bring her up here. You understand?"

"Yeah. I understand," she said, nonchalantly.

Ray slammed the phone down, and threw his hands in the air in despair.

"¡*Demonio*!" he cursed.

What could he do with her? Would he ever have peace and quiet again?[*] Was this flower turning to a thorn in his flesh.

Throughout her life Martha tolerated a love-hate relationship with her mother. She was, at the same time, dependent on and dominated by her. Other times she would try to shake off her influence altogether. But she was never driven away like her father. He had been too mild to oppose his domineering wife. As had been her first husband.

Her mother was overprotective, kept Martha tied to her apron strings. Martha was not allowed to play with other children, nor later to date boys. In fact, rarely in her youth had Martha gone anywhere without her mother's shadow. Even now her old and senile mother dogged her life.

The time had come to say goodbye. Martha looked at her mother lying on the bed. She did not like this anymore than Momma did. But what else could she do?

"I have to go now, Momma."

"Go. Go," Mrs.Beck flung at Martha's feet. "I never want

---

[*] **Raymond** (Ger.), quiet peace.

to see you again."

She didn't deserve this. She hadn't slaved for Martha all her life to end up here. She'd protected her from all the dangers...and this was the thanks she got.

"Momma, don't talk like that."

"You're leaving me here to die. Now that you have a husband you want to be rid of me." Although she was small and in her seventies, a harsh, strong voice grated on Martha's ears.

"I *told* you Momma, I have to find a job when I get to New York. Someone has to look after you. Don't worry, as soon as Ray and I have settled we'll come back for you." She wished this was true, but she knew it could never happen -- would never happen.

"It's a lie!" Mrs.Beck knew the truth. Martha didn't want an old woman around to wreck her future with Ray. It wasn't fair anyway that her daughter should have more success than she had had herself, with two husbands. And her having been a handsome woman in her prime, too. "It's a lie! You want to be rid of me. You're digging my grave before I'm dead. You're killin' me by leaving me here." She began to cry in utter desolation.

She must get out. Before she changed her mind. Before Momma got her way.

Martha studied the pleading figure.

"You're killin' me."

She must get out.

"Goodbye, Momma."

In a last ditch stand, more desperate than Custer's, Mrs.Beck shouted: "Martha! I *order* you not to leave me!"

She opened the door.

"Martha. Don't go. I'm sorry for what I said."

Please don't grovel, thought Sitting Bull.

"Take me with you. I won't be any trouble. I promise you. Please don't leave me. I'm afraid."

The words merely wiped the floor. Everything had been

36

said, pleaded, and thrown at Martha. All in vain.

She stole a final glance at the shriveled monarch, the fading roses on her dress.

"Martha! Martha! Don't go!" Mrs.Beck screamed hopelessly.

Go. Go.

Martha walked out of the prison. Momma was being locked up, as she herself had been locked in her room when young.

She descended the stairs and walked out of the building.

She was cruel. And knew it. She had deserted and exiled her. But it had to be done. The comforting words of the nurse had no effect. She WAS killing Momma.

From an upper window, high above, came a yell that pierced her conscience.

"Goddamn you. Goddamn you. I hope you end up like this, you pagan. I hope someone does this to you."

Martha did not look back.

She had to go on. Ray was her life now. Ray alone. All her security was invested in him. Once she would do anything for Momma. Now Momma was finished. She would never see her again. Ever.

She walked through the grounds of the Nursing Home, tears trickling down her cheeks.

Her black dress flapped in the afternoon chill.

*

Martha's tears had purged Momma from her system. She was never to inquire after her again. The only time she mentioned Momma was when the monthly bill arrived.

She was to start a new life.

Momma was to die.

Bunny was to die.

And even Joe was rekindled to die.

She must start a new life.

The old must die.

DORIS

Firmly ensconced in New York, Martha prepared Ray for his next bigamous marriage -- to Doris Acker.

They caught a train out to Morris County, New Jersey, to go through with the ceremony. Martha watched the event with amusement. When the judge said: "You may kiss the bride," Ray pecked at his new wife's cheek. Doris was not content with his light touch and thrust a big kiss upon him. Just like in the films, Martha thought.

The marriage over, the trio climbed into Doris's estate car, and Ray drove them back to New York. The hot, clear sky was a sure omen of good fortune.

Martha regarded the whole business as sheer farce. How easy it was. One couldn't go wrong.

"Aren't you going to congratulate me, Mrs.Beck?" Doris asked.

Martha had forgotten the tradition. It was one mistake. But only a small one.

"Doris, I think you should call my sister Martha," Ray prompted.

He looked into the rearview mirror and smiled at Martha.

She grinned back.

Martha enjoyed his way of charming Doris. It was amusing when viewed objectively.

"Your car drives very well, Doris." He smiled broadly down at her, beside him.

"*Our* car, darling."

One just had to laugh. Smile at least.

"Goodbye Morristown High School. See you in the fall," Doris said, waving at the building. For the next few months she was as free as the air. "I can't wait to see the expression on my kids' faces when I tell them, 'Boys and girls, from now on your are to address me as Mrs.Fernandez.'" Her face bloomed as large as the white carnations in the bouquet that Ray had bought.

Martha spluttered into laughter.

"What's the matter, Martha?" Doris enquired, squinting over her shoulder.

Martha indicated that she had choked on a chocolate: another of Ray's presents to the bride.

Doris turned back and frowned. She disliked Martha, for she was as fat as a hippopotamus and as greedy as a pig. Now if she was one of her children, she would soon be as slim as a pencil.

And as hungry as her womb?

Her disgust at the glutton quickly dissipated, for her Latin lover was drawing her attention.

"Did they think you would stay a spinster forever?" No reply. Of course not. "Is something wrong, darling? Oh, is it my English? Doesn't that mean 'maiden'?"

Ray was perfect, right down to the last word.

"Oh, you are adorable." Doris turned her innocent eyes up to Ray.

Another lonely heart was temporarily warmed.

And the warmth spread -- to the bathroom.

For when they got back to Ray and Martha's apartment, Doris joyfully went off to scrub and prepare for her first night of married bliss.

Two local men in twenty years of teaching hadn't got her anywhere near marriage. And now, six months with Aunt Carrie and here she had a true Romeo. To quote the immortal Bard:

Jul.   *O gentle Romeo!*
   If thou dost love, pronounce it faithfully:
   Or if thou think'st I am too quickly won,

I'll frown and be perverse and say thee nay,
So thou wilt woo;

Romeo and Juliet, II, ii.

Her young lover was as gentle as a dove and as dear as diamonds to her. Gay as a lark she broke into song.[*]

Oh beautiful for spacious skies
For amber waves of grain
For purple mountains' majesty
Above the fruited plain

America America
God shed his grace on thee
And crown thy good with brotherhood

She stopped.
"Darling, where are you?"

Martha was overjoyed with her new-found occupation. It was more pleasurable than all those monstrosities at the hospital. And so easy.

Already she was rifling through Doris's bag. The notes were just leaving the purse when Doris repeated:

"Where are you?"

"I'm in the living room, darling," Ray called back light-heartedly, and accepted the money Martha handed him.

"Bring me a towel, love."

"You coming out now?"

"No. The bride's going to take a nice soak. But I miss

---

[*] *Jul. It is the lark that sings so out of tune,*
Straining harsh discords and unpleasing sharps.

Romeo and Juliet, III, v.

40

you, sweety. Bring me a towel. We're married, you know."

The randy bitch, Ray thought.

Martha gave Ray a "cute" look.

Never the Twain shall meet in bed. She adoris you.

Her thoughts could be just as witty as anyone's. And as old, tried and common as dirt.

Selecting a towel from the closet, he took it in to her. As they played and splashed, Doris giggling like one of her schoolgirls, Ray ran his eyes up and down the bathing bouquet. She was a round-faced, flat-chested, skinny specimen. The biology class would reject her on sight.

Meanwhile Martha had crossed to the bedroom. She was flipping through the suitcases, searching for valuables.

Having found all she wanted, she retired to their bedroom. Fleecing was like a sixth sense. Simple as ABC.

Ray retreated from the bathroom, much to Doris's displeasure. He made for the bedroom to change his soaking shirt. Lying on the bed beside Martha was a money belt and a couple of rings. He pushed them into the drawer and, smiling, lay down beside Martha. A far greater treasure, for her.

They embraced and made love. Words weren't needed.

Glory glory hallaluuuya
Glory glory hallaluuya
Glory glory hallaluuuya
His truth is marching on

Doris sang as she rubbed herself down.

The bridal suite saw only the bride that night. The carnation was sniffed at. Ray excused himself on the pretext of keeping vigil over his sister, who was feeling unwell. She was having one of her "attacks," and only he knew how to handle her.

The night passed. Doris was not unduly perturbed, although disappointed after her careful preparations.

What was one more night to a virgin of forty-one? A Juliet?

Morning, however, changed that. She hunted through her suitcases for five minutes, but still was unable to find her rings. Then she noticed the missing belt.

That was it. Everything was clear as crystal. She screamed for Ray.

In the kitchen Martha was eating her breakfast. So Doris had finally found out. What did she care? She took another mouthful of the toast and jam.

"Too quick. Too quick," Ray exclaimed, his arms flourishing as he strode into the kitchen, his silk gown flowing behind.

"What's too quick?" she squeezed out.

"You shouldn't have taken her things last night. You should have left them for me to do later. The way I *always* do." Martha's competence as a nurse was not maintained in her new employment. "Now she wants them back. She's furious."

"Where is she?"

"In the bedroom. She's packing."

Martha poured Ray another cup of coffee. Too bad, she thought. Her eyes signaled Ray to sit and calm down.

He sighed torpidly and complied.

Doris appeared in the doorway, dropped her luggage to the floor. She was as white as a sheet. Her summer coat hung askew. Her flowerpot sat propped on the disheveled crop.

"Good morning," Martha said pleasantly, adding two lumps of sugar.

"I'm leaving," growled Doris.

"Already? That was a pretty short honeymoon," Martha responded, as if nothing had happened.

Crossing the kitchen, Martha collected more cream to add to the cluttered table.

"Honeymoon!" choked Doris. "You ought to tell your brother what's supposed to *happen* on a honeymoon." She held her ground: teeth clenched, shoulders hunched, arms rigid by her sides. "Before I go I want my rings and my money belt."

"Your what?"

"My two rings and my money belt with the two thousand dollars in it."

"I don't know what you're talking about."

Doris stepped forward. Bold as brass, her foot pawing the ground as the tension mounted.

"Somebody took them!"

Martha halted the advance. So she wants blood and guts, she thought. She stationed the artillery in front of Doris.

"Now see here. Do you know what happens to people who make false accusations?" she fired.

"I want my rings and my money," Doris retaliated.

"You lower your voice. You're not in your classroom now."

How could anyone possibly win against Martha? Doris looked past to Ray, who had retreated earlier. He had sat at the table where Martha indicated and had not spoken or moved since. He was as silent as the grave.

"You give me back my things or I'll make plenty of trouble for you."

"How dare you talk to my brother like that," intercepted Martha. And she reversed her own experience. "And as for trouble, I wonder what the principal of your school would say if he saw some of those letters you wrote to my brother? I tell you I was *shocked* to see such things from a schoolteacher," she spat out disgustedly. "Don't they have a P.T.A. out there?"

The battle was almost won. The bugle was sounding. Hallaluuuya!

"I'm leaving now. I guess I'm lucky I still have my car keys."

"So who's stopping you?" urged Martha.

"Anyway, I thought you were ill? You look as right as rain to me."

"I am ill. You've made me *sick*."

"Oh!" she huffed. But she quickly regained her lost ground. "Why don't you let your brother talk for himself?" Doris threw her last missile. "You act more like a mother than a sister. Ray, you haven't said one word. Are you afraid of her or something?"

"Get out of here!" Martha screamed.

"I'm going." The wilting flower picked up her baggage, muttering: "This isn't the end. You'll hear from my lawyer."

"Get the hell out of here!" Martha thundered.

The door slammed. The heavens fell.

*

Note: **DORIS** (Celt.), good luck.

She was not to know how lucky she had been to get out alive.

MYRTLE

Silence followed.

Ray was too afraid to speak. Martha's disposal technique had petrified him. He quietly resumed his breakfast.

Having got shot of that one, Martha cleared up the remains. She returned to the kitchen to empty the last of the garbage. St.Martha, the patron of good housewives, had done her job thoroughly.

The first words were spoken.

"Boy is she a slob. It took me half an hour to clean up that bedroom."

Everything was all right now. Ray could move. He could continue his daily business. The powers needed restoring. Call in the repairman. He was he.

Martha entered his workroom and peered over his shoulder. He was preparing her next victim, although he would have liked to have thought -- *their* next victim. No matter what, he intended to have a word in this one.

"Who's that to?"Martha asked.

"A lady from Missouri."

"What do you want to write her for?"

"Because she'll give me four thousand dollars to marry her. Isn't that a good enough reason?"

Martha nodded, for she was reading over the contents. Maybe *he* believes he's Charles Boyer.

"Charles Martin! Where did you think up that name?"

"I didn't. I found it in the directory. Anyway, all she wants is a husband around when the bambino is born so her mother and father won't disinherit her. So I'm using it." Ray laughed as he glanced at the list. "She's through with men."

"Oh," Martha chuckled, "they all say that after they've been knocked up."

"Knocked up?" He still didn't understand all this American slang, as he'd spent the majority of his youth in Spain, learning Spanish slang instead.

"Pregnant."

Although this peach may have wanted a husband for familial reasons, when she saw handsome Charles she would see the man of her fantasies and want him for a true husband. That would always be the case, whatever they might say or write.

"You'd better write her that you'll marry her," Martha dictated. "And tell her that your married sister, Mrs.Beck, will come along with you." That seemed to work okay before.

"Excellent. An excellent idea." Ray smiled, *perfectamente bien*, and then laughed.

The correspondence was started by way of the box number. While it grew Ray performed the rites of his religion, showing Martha the rudimentaries of his practice. She was not particularly interested. She was more excited when her first chance to see the proper New York was planned. They had a bit of money now and some more soon to come, so they could afford to spend a few days, and nights, on the town.

One of the places Ray took her was his favorite night-club in the Bowery, which he had discovered not long after the accident. There they were entertained by aged showgirls who almost matched Martha in size. At first Martha thought it was a dig at her, but her offense was soon allayed by the realization that Ray was a regular.

Also during the waiting period, Martha came to know the deeper side of Ray and learnt to appreciate his individuality. It was so far removed from Boyer's characteristics that she now regarded the comparison as an insult.

Before long they were off to Missouri to marry Myrtle. To elude her parents was all that was required. Another quickie and they would be back in New York.

They were met off the train. Myrtle first drove the three of them to the Justice of the Peace and then to the temporary apartment she had rented for the occasion.

"This is *it*, kids. Not Tara," Myrtle said sarcastically, as she led them into the place. "It's not *even* Little Rock, I'm *afraid*," she added as her eyes panned the place for the second time only.

Myrtle helped Ray off with his jacket, patting down the envelope that was riding from the pocket. She had given it to him in the car straight after the ceremony.

While Martha inspected, Ray continued his fact-finding. The flower of Venus was in her early thirties and maintained a chubby, but well-proportioned, pleasing figure. Her drawbacks were: her head, which was crotched like a yew branch; and her sharp, persistent drawl, which was unbearably nauseous.

"Do your parents have a nice place in Little Rock?" asked Ray.

"Oh, you *bet*. And if it wasn't for a certain *married* son of a *bitch* down there, I'd be home right *now*."

Her matron's round rapidly completed, Martha returned.

"Certainly is a small apartment," she said, slumping onto the couch. There was about as much room to move as between cup and lip.

"Well, it's the *best* I could *do*. I didn't *know* you were coming till *last* week," replied Myrtle. She closed the closet.

"Well, I wish you'd gotten a place with twin beds. I don't like sharing a double bed. Anyhow, not with a woman," Martha quickly added, so as not to be misconstrued.

It wasn't Martha's size that Myrtle disliked, but her patronizing nature.

Myrtle sidled across to Ray and sat, cuddly, on the arm of his chair.

"*Why* you could always sleep in *here*," she said. "After *all*, Charles and I *are* married." And gluing all her attention to Ray, she continued: "You know, you're *much* cuter than your *picture*. No, no, not *cuter*. Let's see...yes, *sexier*." She giggled at her words and squeezed his arm.

She made Martha want to throw up. She really hoped this execution would be swift and sharp. They were married, period.

"I thought you were through with men," said Martha, blunt as a hammer.

"You sound *just like* my *momma*."

In that case it is going to be quick and painless, thought Martha.

"Ohh, *say*, I think I will *phone* momma and *pappa*." She giggled, still their little girl. "Well, *now* that I can produce a *husband*, I might *just* as well start the recon*ciliation*."

"What reconciliation?" Martha asked.

"Well, I'll *give* them the *address*. They *still* don't even know *where I am*..."

Martha's eyes met Ray's. Grateful for the latest piece of information.

"...*Then*, I will introduce them to their *new* son-in-law, *right* on the phone." She giggled and looked desirously at Ray. "My *dark* and *handsome* husband, and *little* old sister *nurse* who has come *all* the way from *New York* to take care of *me* while I have my *baby*."

You must be mad if you think we're staying that long, thought Martha. You can't even see the little bugger yet.

Ray eased back, imagining himself as the doctor supervising the birth. His ambition had been to study medicine, but his father thought his weak son would be bettered by work on the farm. Any book Ray acquired his father destroyed, and tried to beat his quest for knowledge from him. Ray hated his father, for he was refused permission to graduate to high school from the grammar. *El maricón.*

"Wait till tomorrow, Myrtle," Ray said persuasively. "I'm too tired to charm them. I think we should all go to sleep now."

"*Well*! Well, in *that* case I'll just *run down* and *lock up* my new second-hand *car*. I want to fix up something for *Charles* anyway." Myrtle smiled sweetly and slipped round the door. "I'll be *right back, folks*."

Martha rose, refreshed, as soon as the door closed on the love flower.

"Was all the money in the envelope?"

"Every cent. She was as good as her word," Ray beamed.

"Well, now we ought to get out of here. The exploit's over."

"Martha, that's not fair." That was too cruel. "Not fair!" she shouted. "Why wait around till she tells her parents about us. That wasn't part of the deal. We agreed to marriage." And not to bed, or anything else. "I think we ought to get out of here before something happens."

"I'll talk her out of that call in the morning." Ray gestured the idea out of mind.

"Well, I don't like her," was Martha's final point.

"Do you think I do? Jesus, Martha, we are exhausted. At least let's stay the night."

Martha stepped back as the clanging voice of the Southern belle approached.

"God, here she comes again."

Martha was becoming increasingly aggravated. She could not stand the southern drag anymore.

"I don't know what you people are going to do," she said as Myrtle breezed in, "but I'm gonna take a bath."

She swung round and stomped out.

A neatly wrapped parcel was produced from behind Myrtle's back the minute Martha was out of sight. She presented it to her mysterious suitor, sitting quietly in the last rays of sunset.

"*Here*. I bought you a *weddin' present*."

"A present? That wasn't necessary."

"*Well*, for whatever *reasons*, we are *married*. All *signed*, sealed *and* legal, *right*?" She tapped her ring.

"Of course, of course," Ray smiled, and patted her hand. "And I must say you kept your part of the bargain."

"Open up your *present*. I'm *dying* to see it on you. "She clapped her hands and giggled.

"Something to wear?"

"Open it up, *you'll* see."

Ray opened it as slowly and carefully as she had wrapped it.

"A wig," he announced.

"*No*, a *hairpiece*," proudly enlightened Myrtle.

Neither was correct. It's real term was a toupee.

"Oh thank you, darling."

"Come *on, try* it on. There's a *mirror* in the bedroom. Come along *there*," said the shining evergreen excitedly.

In front of the mirror, Ray sat admiring his new image. The hairpiece was even a close color to his own near-black.

"Oh, *darlin'*, you look *irrrresistable*!" squealed Myrtle with delight.

"It's not bad, is it? It blends well," said Ray, smoothing down the straggling hairs.

"Ohhh, *yes*." She giggled.

"You're pretty clever, darling. How did you know it would suit me?"

"*Well*, I took *your* photo along to the *store*, and *they* told me *this* one would be *just right*."

She rested her chin on his shoulder and admired them both in the mirror.

"And the color, darling?" Ray quizzed.

"Oh, *that* was *easy*. I *guessed*. You being of *Spanish blood* an' all. It *had* to be *black*." She smiled swankily at the glass.

She knew she'd done right to choose Charles. He was the only one she could have fallen for amongst the candidates.

50

All the rest looked too square for her.

"*See*, it's *all gone* now," she said, pointing to his no-longer visible scar or receding hairline. It also made his narrow but regular features broader. And emphasized the oliveness of his complexion, removing any trace of swarthiness.

"I wonder why I never thought of that before?"

The accident that had produced the scar happened while Ray was working on an oil tanker. He was struck on the head by a falling hatch. It had injured the frontal lobes of the brain, leaving a three-inch scar high on his forehead. It was on his discharge from hospital in Curaçao that he had noticed his whole personality had changed. People who knew him well agreed. He would not do things he had done before. For example, he shied away from violence where before he might have been attracted. No one would have thought that he had been commended for his courage with the British Intelligence in Gibraltar during World War II. And what was once a woman-shy man was now a gigolo.

As they both admired the black cover, Martha waddled in from the bath.

"What's going on in here?" she quacked.

"*How* do you *like* your brother with his *new little addition*?" said Myrtle conceitedly, unable to contain her enthusiasm.

"What? A wig?" Martha said flatly.

How it changed him, she thought. Sure he still looked handsome, but it wasn't her little ray of sunshine.

Like all the other flowers whose gardens Ray had trampled, Martha could not have helped but notice his prominent scar. But she dismissed it as a war wound, since Ray often boasted of his prowess in the field.

"It's *not* a *wig*. It...*that* is a *hairpiece*, Martha. *I* think *he* looks *deeevine*," breathed Myrtle.

"Where did you get it?" demanded Martha.

"I, uh, bought it in New York before we left," stammered

51

Ray as he sprang to his feet, warding off Myrtle's reply with his eyes. "I wanted to surprise you. I thought it would be...amusing to change my appearance a little."

Very clever, darling. But don't wear it too often, Martha thought.

It annoyed Martha that Ray was restoring his Boyer image with the toupee. First Charles. Now the hair. He'd be off to Hollywood next. She didn't want a celluloid negative in *her* epic.

"Well, it doesn't look too bad," Martha said. "I'll just have to get used to it, I guess." And quickly changing the subject: "Well, I think we should all go to bed now. Myrtle, why don't you take a nice hot bath?"

"Now, *what* is *that* supposed to mean? *What*, do I *smell* or something?"

You smell all right, sister.

"No, no, no," Ray cut in. "My sister didn't mean anything. She's so used to her hospital routine." He patted Myrtle's baby face as he passed. "Well, I'm going to make up my bed." He inclined his head to each. "Goodnight, ladies." Ray cut out.

"I didn't mean that the way it sounded," Martha corrected, pulling down the sheet. "It's just that there's nothing better than a good soak to really relax you. Why don't you try it?"

That should work.

"Maybe I *will*. I do *feel* a little peaky."

It did work. Myrtle went for a bath.

The idea of sending Myrtle off to bathe had come from the Doris chapter. However, Martha intended to spend the stolen time with Ray's valuables and not with Myrtle's.

Ray was making up his bed on the couch when Martha entered.

"She's in the bathtub," she whispered, putting her arms around him.

"Not now, I'm tired." He disentangled himself from the bear hug. "She might come in."

52

"You didn't care with Doris Acker."

"We made plenty of mistakes that night." He shrugged her off again to finish his bed. He must be authoritative this time. "Now please go to bed. Keep your hands off her things. This whole thing must be handled with a little *savoir faire*. And you don't have it. You understand?"

He turned, slipping off his waistcoat. She had gone.

Straight to bed. She wanted to make love, but he had rejected her.

She lay awake, waiting for Myrtle to come from the bath.

"Martha. You up?" Myrtle whispered when she came in .

No reply.

"Good."

She turned and crept out with a giggle.

The sexploit began.

She tiptoed across to Ray, who sat up at her entry. He stared at the bouncing balls in the flimsy nightgown that toppled towards him.

"Myrtle, what are you doing here?"

"I *wanted* to *talk* to you."

Her voice was a few tones quieter than usual, but it lost none of its characteristic drawl.

"What's so important?" Ray asked.

"*Well*, I can't *help* wondering *why* you *lied* to your sister about the *hairpiece*."

"Please understand, darling, my sister and I are very close, and I think she would have been hurt that someone else had given me something so personal."

"Oh, I *see*."

"Okay. Go to bed now, my dear. We'll talk about everything else in the morning."

No sooner had Martha got out of bed than she had to climb back again before Myrtle came creeping in.

Everyone slept.

Myrtle awoke after an hour and crept in again to Ray. She wasn't going to sit beneath the tree pricking the leaves, as Phaedra had done when she waited for Hippolytus. She ran her hands over his thick bushy chest. He was adorable. A live teddy bear.

"Martha, Martha, I told you," Ray said dreamily.

"It's not *Martha*."

Ray opened his eyes.

"Oh. Did I call you Martha?" he said innocently.

"I *can't* sleep." She sat on the bed and tried to hug the toy. "I thought *maybe* we could just *talk*."

"I told you, we'll talk in the morning."

"Okay. Let's not talk."

She tried to get aboard him. He rolled her off.

"What's *wrong*? Can't you *see* I'm *crazy* bout you?" she said, closing in.

"My sister's in there," riposted Ray.

"Oh, she's *fast* asleep. Come *on*, honey bun."

She curled onto the bed beside him and put his hand round her waist.

"Why don't you *explore* a little bit? Oh *honey*, *don't* be so *shy* . You *can't* get me into *any* more trouble than *I'm* in, *even* if you tried."

La zorra.

"Not now," Ray parried.

But she was gaining the upper hand.

"Sssss. *You* act like a *lil* ole *virgin* boy."

"Sshhh," he countered.

"That *sister* of *yours*, *mothers* you *too* much. Don't you *want* me to be *your* lil ole southern *mammy*? Come *on*, honey bun, you *want* some *sugar*?"

She coaxed his head into her breasts. He was overpowered by the perfume of the bloom.

"Mmn. That's nice," he mumbled.

But he sensed Martha's eyes upon the scene, and with a final struggle, pulled himself out.

"Go to bed now. Go to sleep. Stay there and promise you'll stay there," Ray commanded.

"Oh, *you're* a meany. *Ohooo, meany, meany.* Right, I'll *go*."

"Go. Go. *Vete*."

Martha beat Myrtle back to their bed. This time she was ready to talk, to stop these moonlight flits. She envied the little attention Ray had paid Myrtle, for she herself had received none that night.

"What's the matter? Can't you sleep? You woke me up," Martha said snappily.

"Oh, I'm *sorry*. I *guess* I'm just *restless*."

"Want a sleeping pill? I've got some."

"*Have* you any *other* kind?" smirked Myrtle.

"Whadda ya mean?"

"*Agh* never mind. *You* wouldn't, *you're* too *square*."

Myrtle lay back sighing with the memory of all the other beaux whose beds she'd climbed into. Charles was like Everest -- Unconquerable.

"You sigh a lot, don't you?" Martha bitched. "In nursing school they taught us that people who sigh a lot are unstable. Is that your problem?"

"*No. I's just* thinkin' about your *brother*, and *how handsome* he looks in that hairpiece I gave him." She turned towards Martha, giggling, her hand covering her mouth. She could be nasty too. "He *lied* to ya."

"I don't believe it. He never lies to me." Or does he? Martha sat up, struggling to control her quivering body and mind.

"*I* think he's a little bit *afraid* of *you*. It's *probably* why he *never* married *before*," Myrtle said, and giggled. "I bet *I'm* gonna have to *show* him what to *do*." Her eyes gleamed at the idea.

"You must think you're an authority." Big head.

"Well, I *am* pregnant." Fat ass.

"Not only are you pregnant, you're repulsive. You're the

55

hottest bitch I've ever seen," declared Martha, nauseated. She had had her fill of this southern lass and her snide comments.

"And I *don't* have to take *that* from *you*," was the instantaneous retort as Myrtle shot up, and launched herself at the Mississippi steamer: "And *let* me tell *you* something. *I'm* in *love* with your brother. And *if* we *decide* to make a *go* of this *marriage*, which *I* think we'll *do*, and *sooner* than you *think*, *why* we'll get out of *here* fore you can say *Jack Robinson. We* will go to Little Rock. *Why*, as a matter of *fact*, I will make *all* the arrangements on the *phone* with my *pappy* tomorrow. *Charles* will fit *right* in with us. *He* has *style. You* can go *right* back to *that* -- that *hospital* of yours, where *you* can *boss* everybody around. *Now* I'm going back to *my* husband." With her monologue neatly packed and sealed, she swung from the bed and dashed out to the lounge.

Martha had no time to reply and no opportunity throughout to get a word in edgeways. That girl had nearly breathed her last word the way she went on.

Martha could have cheerfully killed Myrtle, *right* there.

Prompted by her thought, Martha got up and took a handful of pills from her purse. She slipped them into her gown pocket. Just in case. Never had she met such a person in her life. She was worse than a skunk.

Ray rushed into the room. He would stand for no nonsense tonight.

"Damn it, Martha. What have you been saying to Myrtle?" he roared.

"Well, we've been talking about quite a few things," she replied pertinently.

"Well, what?"

"Well, mostly she's worried whether you can screw or not."

"She didn't talk about anything like that," he said, swinging his hand through the air to denounce the idea.

"She certainly did," Martha affirmed.

"Goddamn it, trouble again." He flung his hands up despairingly, turned and strode away. "You see you should have stayed in New York. I never should have let you come."

"Sure. Then you could do what she wants."

"I got one woman carrying on in there, another carrying on in here. Christ almighty. I'm earning my four thousand tonight!"

He clapped his head against the wall.

"Now look. This is the third time she came to me," he specified to straighten out the incident. "If I wanted to screw her she would be satisfied by now. I want her to go to sleep."

"Is that all you want from her?" Martha sought cautiously.

"That's all, for Chrissake."

"Here." Martha scooped some pills out of her pocket. "Give her these. Tell her they were the kind of pills she was asking for," she said, meeting his eyes. He was hers alone. And would remain so while she was around to supervise.

Myrtle cast a suspicious glance over the pills Ray handed her. But there were no questions. She gulped them down.

Almost immediately she fell asleep. Much to Ray's relief - - and to Martha's.

Now there were no barriers. Martha went to Ray. He submitted to save a further scene.

Finally, they all slept, peacefully.

Morning and Myrtle felt ill. The pills had had an adverse effect. She couldn't move from the couch where she'd spent the night. She called Ray to her side and stammered out how sick she was feeling.

Martha was annoyed at being lumbered with this burden. She would have been only too glad to leave the moaning Myrtle to recover alone, but Ray's compassion demanded patience. He couldn't leave Myrtle by herself. First he would put her on the bus to Little Rock, and only then would Martha and he drive back to New York in their newly acquired Ford.

Martha sneered that he could do just that, but *she* was staying in bed till they'd gone. She couldn't bear to hear another squeak from the grizzly.

In all the hubbub Martha had forgotten to inquire why Ray had lied about the hairpiece. By the time she remembered they'd already departed, and so she decided to keep it to herself.

Little resistance was shown as Ray put Myrtle in the car and started for the bus depot. She was too groggy to know what was happening. All she could do was moan.

"Ohhhh, oh, I'm *so* sick. I...I don't feel any *better*, Charles," she moaned.

"By the time you get to Little Rock, you'll feel much better. Don't worry. Relax."

Ray tried to comfort her. To no avail. What had happened to the cherub of yesterday? He was scared. They had only given her a few barbiturates. He couldn't understand this prolonged reaction.

"You must have been allergic to them," he blurted, spilling his thoughts tactlessly.

"Oh, Charles. Does that mean I'm gonna die from all those pills?" she asked, frightened out of her life. She'd never felt so ill.

"No, Myrtle. Don't be silly. You relax."

Putting her on the bus was more difficult. He had to take care that none of the other passengers noticed the pale color of the female, or heard her sickly moans. He would say the heat was affecting her if anyone queried.

He sat next to her in the waiting bus and made last minute attempts to calm her.

She was still unable to fully comprehend the situation, but sensed that she was being abandoned.

"*Why* are you putting me all *alone* on the bus?" she whispered. "I'm *so* sick. Ohhhh, I don't want to go by *myself*."

"I told you before. Now listen. I'll call your mother and father," he affirmed, "and tell them to meet the bus. Then I'll drive your car down with all the rest of your things. Okay?"

"Please, *please*, don't bring *her* along," she cried.

"I'll come all by myself. Just the two of us," he mumbled absently.

"Ohhhh, I feel so *terrible*, Charles," she moaned as a fresh attack of pain began.

Ray had to go, before it was too late. He towered like a redwood over the weeping willow.

"Look, there's no time now. You'll be off soon. I gotta go. Go to sleep. Okay? Go to sleep."

He patted her cheek and escaped from the bus to the safety of his car.

As he drove back, he hoped she would arrive safely. A long sleep would do her good, he thought. Martha could have told him that a long sleep was deadly. Particularly as neither knew of Myrtle's liver complaint. Being pregnant wouldn't help either.

By the time the bus reached Little Rock, Myrtle had keeled over in her seat.

She was dead.

A wreath of myrtle was lain on her grave.

EVELYN

Within the week they were back on the road. This time to Pittsfield, Massachusetts, to visit a Miss Evelyn Long. Her letters had indicated she was a prosperous thirty-nine-year-old. And when she had sent a photograph of her home, a mansion by a lake, it clinched the trip.

Martha forbade marriage. Money and money alone must stay in the forefront of their minds.

On arrival they were disillusioned to find that although the white house was owned by Evelyn, it operated as a select boarding house in the summer season. And naturally they had descended during the peak. The summer school at Tanglewood meant that musicians fully booked her house. Ray could just be accomodated, but Martha had to be booked into a nearby motel, much against her wishes. Martha was particularly sore that she had been deceived by the twenty-year-old photograph of the house. To Ray it meant nothing, for many women acted similarly, usually with photographs of themselves.

For the first time, Ray was free for a few hours out of the twenty-four -- the dark hours. He worked his powers of Voodoo upon Evelyn. The flowers of evil opened into an affair by night.

Evelyn seemed satisfactory. She was warm, friendly and pleasant. She led a cosy life. The returns from the house were adequate to live on. But she had no substantial amounts to be taken. Perhaps he should settle down with her. Marry her. Would Martha take the hint and leave? Or would he have to resort to bribery?

His first story to Martha was that Evelyn's money would take time to obtain. Till the end of the season at least.

Martha was resolute in her demands for a return to New York. She wanted a little home of her own and she wanted it now. It was no good Ray telling her this woman was rich. They would have to find more money elsewhere. Motel commuting was unbearable and expensive.

Ray was just as resolute in his demands that they stay. He was dominating this situation and meant to enjoy the power he held. They needed a vacation away from the hot city. Why shouldn't they take advantage of the occasion? He even turned Martha's persistent plea for a house to his benefit, by saying: "People who have houses in the suburbs are supposed to take summer vacations. So, we're having ours."

But she didn't have her house, so why should she laze around here.

Clearly Martha was hating every minute. Each morning she would rise early, throw on her clothes and rush over to the mansion for breakfast. And each evening she would leave as late as possible.

Each morning. Each evening. Each morning. Each evening. The routine was tiring her, wearing her patience. She could not stand much more.

Each day they lay by the lake, bathing and picnicking.

One day as she set off from the motel for their tryst, Martha determined that decisions would be made that day. Somehow or other they would return to New York -- with money or without.

It had been apparent to Evelyn all morning that Martha was discontent. Her affable chatter had received no response. When she opened the picnic basket for a pre-lunch snack, mainly for her visitor's benefit, Martha refused.

Martha refused! Rarely did she reject food.

Evelyn shrugged, and nibbled on alone. Her appetite whetted, she joined Ray for a swim.

"Here I come!" she broadcast.

The beating heat of the noonday sun made Martha turn aside her magazine and brood. The heat. What were they doing now? The heat. The echoes of their laughing sounds playing in the water, played on her mind. The heat. It wasn't right that a woman should own so much, and all the men. Couldn't she find another among the bloody band? The heat. Can't she keep her hands off him for a minute? The heat.

They emerged from the lake, back to Martha's outstretched sphere.

"It was wonderful, Martha. You should really try it," Ray said, grabbing a towel.

"Yeah, maybe I will."

Ray looked so handsome in his striped bathing suit. Those other days when he wore his white beach robe he looked much more chic. Valentino and his beloved, Martha. She was envious that another woman could study his well-built body so closely. Did she study more than that at night? Martha shuddered. It had been two weeks since *she* had felt his warmth.

Her thoughts were halted by the carved body and stone-etched face of Evelyn. The frustrated bitch was speaking to her.

"I don't think you're having a very good time, Martha."

"Well, since you ask," Martha snapped back, sitting up, I don't like staying at the motel by myself."

She had said it before and she would say it again. Evelyn supplied the same answer every time.

"I know, and I do feel terrible," she said amiably, "but this is the last week at Tanglewood. And then everybody will go home and I'll have room enough for you, too." And, as always, she added, "I'm so lucky I have room enough for Ray."

Bitch. You evil bitch. Why do you taunt me? Stop rubbing his back. He's not a child. He can dry himself.

"Well, I have slept in the same room as my brother before," Martha pronounced sulkily .

"It was long ago when we were still children," Ray said,

and laughed half-heartedly.

Wipe that stupid grin off your face, Martha thought. And take that idiotic cigar out of your mouth.

"Shall we have our lunch?" said Evelyn, cheerfully changing the subject to Martha's favorite. "Don't know about you two, but I'm starved."

Again Martha rejected the food. The sun. She was in no mood to eat. The sun. She rose to her feet.

He doesn't give a damn. Pays no attention to me. Like home. He likes the cow, that's it. More than a job. Eyes. Can't even meet my eyes. Why do I have to be the ugly duckling?

"Well, I'm hot. I think I'll go in and cool off."

She slipped out of her robe, dumped it, and waddled to the water in her tutu bathing suit. The sugar plump fairy.

"Yeah, go ahead. Evelyn and I, uh, will get the picnic ready."

The fakeness rang in her ears as she hit the water.

You bastard Ray. You bloody brute. Even you. Et tu.

Evelyn was constantly worried about Martha. She felt sorry for her. It wasn't right that she should have to read magazines for her quota of amours. Of course she was fat, with legs cultivated in a forest, but surely someone could love her?

She watched Martha vent her anger on the water, trying to stamp it underfoot.

"I'm really sorry she doesn't seem to be having a good time," Evelyn said to Ray, as he stretched out on the blanket.

"Don't be silly," Ray reproved jokingly.

"I really do wish I could do something to please her."

"She's moody. It's not your fault. She's enjoying it out there."

She certainly did look like a duck taking to water, thought Evelyn.

"Want to know something?" he said quietly.

"What?"

"You lie down here and no one can see you."

"That's a fascinating piece of information," she said, coyly regarding him through her eyelashes. "What's that supposed to mean?"

"Why don't you try it and find out?"

> O! beware, my lord, of jealousy;
> It is the green-ey'd monster *

"All right," she grinned. "I will."

She shrugged Martha out of her mind and lay back for the stars and stripes.

She was satisfied with his flag, and his pole. Perhaps she should settle down with him. Marry him. Her reason for joining the club was to meet other companions than the overly serious musicians who frequented her place. Marriage could be right with Ray.

Martha's lungs flagged. She had stomped around enough, almost out of her depth. The water was a balm. She was appeased. Maybe now she would turn back for some lunch, before that greedy pig of a woman stuck her big snout into it.

Where were they?

A streak of lightning zipped through her body.

!arhhhhhhHHHHHHHHHHHHHHHHHHH

Hell burst inside her.

"You promised! You promised!" she screamed.

¡Que Diable!

"What is it?"

"She saw us," replied Evelyn.

---

* *Iago. Othello, III, iii.*

They were up in a flash.

"Look!"

"You promised! You promised!"

The two figures blurred before her. The land was one haze. She was out of her mind.

She turned and swam away from it all. Swam. Further. And swam. Further. Out and out.

"Come back!" Ray yelled.

"Ray, Ray make her come back!"

"Martha, please come back!"

"What's the matter with her? I can't understand it."

"Martha, please, please come back!"

"She's out too far and she doesn't swim that well," Evelyn pleaded.

¡Condenación!

A moment of urgency hit Ray. It wasn't a joke. She would do it for him. Once again he realized how much this woman, this jewel would suffer for him. The only one who would. The true one.

"Oh my God, Martha. Martha!"

He ran into the water, bellowing:

"Martha! I'm coming!"

And swam for dear life.

She had floundered. She sunk. Surfaced. Sunk. Surfaced.

Memories surrounded her. Prodded her body.

RAY: You can't bring the old lady. Get rid of her. Choke her.

MOMMA: Martha, what's the matter with my little girl?

MARTHA: Oh, stop it, Momma!

MYRTLE: You sound *just like* my *momma*.

"Pappa. Momma."

MOMMA: Goddamn you. Goddamn you. I hope you end up like this.

RAY: Will you still commit suicide for me?

...Please save me, Ray.

MYRTLE: *How handsome* he looks in that hairpiece *I* gave
    him. He *lied* to ya.
JOE: I'll always be faithful, my love.
EVELYN: I'm so lucky I have room enough for Ray.
    "Help. Help."
MYRTLE: Come *on* honey bun, you *want* some *sugar*.
    Her breasts bouncing into his mouth
RAY: I'm not going back to that hot city.
    The naked woman jumping up
    The naked woman
EVELYN: Here I come.
                Here I come,
                Here I come
    "You crazy little fool. I didn't mean it Martha. I didn't
mean it," beseeched Ray.
    The montage whirled into one mass.

    Ray held her up and wildly planted kisses on her face.
    "You all right?"
    He helped her swim back to the shore.
    "Are you all right?"
    Martha sobbed as he hugged and kissed her every few feet
gained.
    "Hold on, hold on."
    He dragged her out of the water after him.
    "You crazy fool."
    He held her by the shoulders and shook her.
    "You crazy fool. I didn't mean it."
    They embraced.
    "I didn't mean it."
    They sank to the ground. More kisses.
    "Crazy little fool."
    Evelyn was completely bewildered. She bent down on the
bank, splashed her cold face and tussled-blonde mop. The
catalyst stood benumbed, watching the performance. Her
pleas for Ray to act had not anticipated this kind of brother-

66

sister relationship. It was incestuous.

They should leave as soon as possible was Evelyn's first thought. She told them of her request calmly and amicably, disguising her deep hurt. Her upbringing had not accounted for perversions, nor perverted relationships.

Ray thought so too, on both counts.

Informing Martha of their hasty departure, Ray hoped would provoke her to speak again. Calm, not charm, was required in his approach.

"Don't be angry with me. I'm the one who should be angry," he said, rapping his knuckles on his chest.

No good.

Ray paced round the room, stopped at the window. Outside it was the same as any other day. One wouldn't have guessed that anything had changed.

His eyes focused on the spot in the lake where Martha had slubbered in distress, then strayed to the figure of Evelyn talking below to a guest. Turning, he crossed back to the seated stone in the crown.

"Do you realize that with your stupid jealousy you could have gotten me into trouble? Huh? You want me to go to jail?"

He sat opposite, his eyes begging for an answer.

Martha broke her gigantic stare and spoke bluntly.

"I'd rather see you in jail than on that blanket making love to another woman."

¡Ay! She speaks.

"You know you'd go to jail too," he said, grinning.

She rolled her answer around in her mouth before replying:

"Knowing that you'd be locked up away from other women, I'd go too."

The upturned corners of his mouth faltered, but the smile was sustained.

He believed her. She'd go to any lengths to keep him. It was true, he knew he'd been taking her for granted. Whether she'd meant to commit suicide or simply use the attempt as a bait for his love, he just couldn't let her drown. No one else jeopardized their life for him. Besides, his powers, although capable of murder, were not designed for such ends. They were to enable him to get a hold on women. Now she had a hold over him. He'd have to accept the fact, and her. She would have to remain the jewel in his locket.

"Well, I think we'd better get you that house in the suburbs. We'll have to scrape together all we've got to do it, darling."

Martha smiled. She was glad that her attempt had been successful. The intent had been greater this time. Before, she had rarely achieved her aims so successfully, regardless of whether she'd actually tried or merely pretended the suicides.

Her eyes met his. In the screens she re-enacted the first time in her Mobile kitchen. There she had been bewitched by the inamorato, her Valentino.

Her image of the star was unfortunate for it had held other connotations this afternoon. She hoped it would soon fade.

Deep down, she knew it would recur.

JANET

Martha and Ray were nearly broke. The renting and installation of themselves in Martha's new home on Long Island had swallowed most of their resources. They were eating into their final bag of dimes.

But at long last she had her dream boy and her dream house. Nothing, but nothing, would divide the security. That was a certainty. Martha would do everything in her power to maintain this position.

The latest list appeared in her hands, and she selected the next victim. The most suitable was one Janet Fay, a fifty-six-year-old widow. That was settled as far as she was concerned. Now Ray would be incapable of mixing business and pleasure. She couldn't picture a charmer like him making a sexual play for an elderly hag.

Almost single-handed Martha penned the introductory letter, although Ray was allowed to do the mechanical part as a benevolent but necessary concession.

He bore her whims silently, not wanting to cross her course and cause a further upset.

The rolling stone was halted to gather.

They sat on the rock and waited.

Days passed. Nothing. Women were usually so delighted to receive a letter from Raymond Fernandez (or Charles Martin) that they replied by return while the intoxication was strongest.

Without fail, every morning, Martha had upped and collected the letters no sooner had the postman pushed them into the mailbox.

Bills. Always bills. No answer from Janet.

"Nope."

Ray looked up from the story he was reading.

This was stupid.

Fay had been on the list for as long as he could remember. He'd have thought the old fool would have jumped when she finally got a nibble.

"You shoulda let me write the letter by myself," Ray said. "Maybe it wasn't convincing enough."

Martha paid no attention, she was running through the mail. Had she been listening she would have ignored the indirect insult.

Certain minor things she didn't care to lower her pride over. It was major humiliations, concerning her emotions, that plunged her pride to rock bottom.

"We still haven't paid December for my mother," she said. "This is the third one in the last two weeks. They're getting nasty."

"God, we could sure use a good seven or eight thousand," Ray muttered to himself.

"Hold on awhile. She's out of town. She'll answer." Martha put the post aside.

"Yeah, maybe. In case," he said, subconsciously burying himself in the magazine again, "I'd better get back in touch with that Downing woman."

"No!"

Martha rose from the couch and slouched in her sloppy housecoat to the table.

"I'm not going to Michigan." That was definite. "Besides, she's too young." That's what she was definite about.

"What do you mean, too young?" Ray smirked.

"You know what I mean."

Martha recalled Ray's head buried in that southern whore's bosom, Ray tugging on that statue's bathing suit. And for extra measure she concocted a scene with Ray and Doris in the bath, trying a hot tap variation in bathplug major.

"Don't eat candy at ten o'clock in the morning!" Ray yelled. He was getting increasingly annoyed with Martha recently. Why was it he'd got out the wrong side of bed that morning and almost every other morning for the past week?

"It's because you're making me nervous!" Martha screamed back.

"*You're* nervous! How do you think *I* feel, sitting around here day after day? I've even taken to reading these stupid magazines of yours."

He slung the **True Confessions** he had been reading at her feet as she sat. His comment stung. The magazines weren't so stupid to Martha. They had filled all those lonely days and nights of her previously empty life. Some of the stories she almost knew backwards, had lived every moment of the heroine, had felt every touch of the handsome lover. It was too late now to break the habit. And losing herself in the romance still cheered her when depressed.

"I thought it was what you wanted," Martha said, her voice trembling.

"*I* wanted! *You* wanted this house." He jabbed at his chest and then lurched from his seat. "You almost drowned yourself to get it, remember? I suppose the next thing you'll do is cut your wrists...or go out and get a job."

"Stop it!"

"Or turn on the gas like the first time."

"Stop it." Martha stood up, swaying on the edge of the cliff of tears. "Maybe you want me dead."

Yes, no, he didn't know.

"Dead. I'm dead. Finished," he said, quietening. His tempers were hot, but were quickly dispelled. He parted the net curtains. "They call this place Valley Stream. What a joke. One little jail after another, with ten feet of grass between them. Valley Stream," he choked. "I hate it here. *Es una casucha.*"

Both remembered the jails of their youth -- their homes. Ray also recollected the jail he was unfairly sent to when as a teenager he stole some chickens. His father had refused to celebrate Thanksgiving and had suggested that his son procure his own chicken if he wished to honor the holiday. Ray had done so, from the local farmer, by night. His punishment: sixty days. And the next, and last, jail, just after the accident. His minor stealing offense had involved some government-stamped bed linen, which he had kleptomaniacally (for he knew it was unsalable) lifted from his ship. Customs had stopped him. One year. Later reduced to six months.

"We could go someplace else," Martha said.

The trapped cats were more docile. They had bared their teeth. The lioness sat. The king was still wary.

"Where could we go? We can't even afford this rotten little house," Ray said disgruntledly.

"I could go back to nursing." A horrible thought, a last resort, but a possibility not to be ruled out.

"How we gonna live on that?" Ray turned from the window and rolled back his fallen shirt sleeves. "Besides, no woman's going to support *me*. No, I have to go back to work, and I can't invest everything in one old lady you choose for me. Besides, I detest old ladies. I'm going to write to Delphine Downing today."

They had come the full circle.

"Look, I told you, when we get enough money we can get married and go someplace far away from here. Settle down, someplace nice. *Not* Valley Stream."

"When?" Martha asked. Could they maybe go to Martha's Vineyard? She'd always wanted to go there, since she was a child.

"If you do as I say, very soon."

His hands on her face were so gentle. His eyes so kind. Oh she did love him, so much. If only that woman would...

"Maybe Fay will answer," she said.

"Yeah, maybe. But if not, we go to Michigan. If you love me you'll do it," he caressed.

Martha yielded with a nod, and accepted the matador's kiss.

Her appearance was becoming messy. She looked like a

ragged bundle of firewood. The desire to tell her what a ghastly sight she presented was as strong as ever. But Ray never would. It was against his nature. Nor would he disclose her chronic halitosis. He was not a cruel man. How could he marry her though? He would stall longer yet. The sad truth was he just could not grab the bull by the horns. But when the time to do so arose, it would be with a clear conscience, for he had warned her at the start that it was unnatural for him to stay with one woman in one place. Why then was she still so possessive?

Martha's mind was concentrating on Janet Fay.

Write, you bitch. Write.

Janet would have done so right away if it had not been for her closest friend Lucy. She had shown her the letter from forty-five-year-old Charles Martin and had been advised to restrain her over-eagerness and let a week elapse before replying.

An earlier experience ought to have taught her a lesson. She had corresponded through a lonely heart's club a year previous and had been swindled of a few hundred dollars by a charmer. She had since been advised to cease these childish pranks by her daughter Sara and son-in-law Albert.

But Janet was overwhelmed by the letter. How could Charles be harmful? He sounded so gentle and refined. Look how he lived with his sister in a cute little chalet-house. What a nice picture they had sent of it. And his sister, so cute, and a nurse. And it was marvelous how it had been Martha who had picked her from the list.

Janet was completely taken in. She barely managed to wait a week before posting her reply.

"Thank God," said Martha coming into the kitchen, waving the letter from Albany. "Fay's finally replied."

"Let *Charles* open it."

"Saturday today, that means a week and a half," Martha

said to herself, dropping back in her chair.

After reading the letter, Ray grinned and passed it across to Martha, without comment.

She propped the two sheets up against the marmalade pot and read while she ate, taking in as much as was possible in one go.

Dear Charles,

I was all excited to receive your sweet letter. It is so nice to write to someone who is such a good man and who has such a wonderful sister as you have.

The picture is lovely. Sometimes I wish I still had mine. When my husband died, Sara, my daughter, and her husband Albert, were so kind and helped me to sell my house and belongings. The ten thousand dollars I got means that I can

"Ten thousand! Just what the doctor prescribed," Martha said, laughing. "I told ya it was worth waiting."

"Well, she *says* she's got it," Ray cautioned. "But what they write is often a little different from the truth."

Martha averted her eyes, remembering her own little white lies.

"See," Ray recommenced with an air of conceit, "my powers make them reveal exactly what I wanna know."

"Yeah." But aren't you forgetting I wrote it, love. "Well, what next? Do we visit her straightaway?"

"Of course, my darling," he smiled.

Martha returned her eyes to the letter.

helped me to sell my house and belongings. The ten thousand dollars I got means that I can live quite comfortably alone in my hotel apartment. It is not very big, but I do not need too much space to do the things I have to do.

But I do miss the company of the late Mr. Fay. He

was such a wonderful man.

Now I have a wonderful friend in Lucy. But she is married and has alot to do, so I am looking for some companions who I can write and share my life with.

I hope I have not hurt your feelings by taking so long to reply, but I have not been in good health of late.

I must close now, dear Charles, or else I will be late for church.

I will pray for you and your sister.

God bless you both

Janet J. Fay

Ray watched her eyes dart back and forth. When they halted, he said:

"Let's write that we'll visit in a week. Say, we just *happen* to be passing by on our way to...I don't know." He took a bite of his toast and munched on. "Pittsfield!"

To be reminded of the Evelyn experience was not a pleasant thought for Martha. But her delight at Janet's unintentional good news rapidly stifled her reproaches.

"We're gonna spend the Christmas vacation with relations. Aunt *Evelyn*." Ray sat back, pleased with the idea.

Martha smiled to hide her underlying thought and tucked into her breakfast. Talking through a crammed mouth she said, upon reflection:

"Wouldn't it make more sense to say, on our way back, *after* the vacation?"

"We need the money as soon as possible, Martha. You know that," he said, tapping his knife on the coffeepot.

"Just think though." She swallowed. "At Christmas all her relatives will be there. And that's the last thing we want -- a family reunion. It'd be better to go after they've gone."

"All right, if you think so."

"Make it New Year. Lonely people are *always* lonelier

then," she informed.

"Very good, Martha. But it's a bit late."

"And it'd make a deeper impression on her," she forced. "New Year's always good for new contacts."

Underneath, Martha knew that what she'd said was true. She had experienced it many times herself.

"We still need money *before* Christmas," Ray stressed.

"Oh, I've got some of Myrtle's rings I was gonna keep for myself," she admitted. "I'll sell them. That should tide us over." She smiled at her witticism.

"Fine. Fine, Martha." He smiled in return and sipped his coffee. "We'll have a quiet Christmas, and then back to work."

He felt content. Even the prospect of a Christmas alone with Martha was undaunting, for he would soon be off to work. Life was so boring when no job was in hand. He was happiest when plotting the victims, and maneuvering in for the kill. His every thought was for the goal, rarely a thought for the gaol.

He broke his gaze from the rain that was beating against the window.

"You'd better write back today. And don't forget to pray for the poor soul afterwards," Martha quipped.

Ray spluttered into his coffee, and removing the cup, said: "Okay, I'll also put off Delphine, darling."

"Amen."

"Now look what you've done. All over my dressing gown."

Martha smiled through her jammed teeth, then added: "I'll help you change, if you want."

After Janet's letter was scribed, Ray spread it flat on the table before him. Sprinkling it with a little of one of his sacred powders, he rubbed the grains into the paper with his middle finger. Then he sat, his eyes fixed on:

and cast his hypnotic influences upon her.

He called on his gods, who were represented in the room by the images of his former religion, Catholicism, to make the prey more susceptible to his persuasions.

Encircling him on the walls and furniture, as he sealed the envelope, were paintings of Christ and statues of the Saints. On his small altar were erected various crucifixes, candles, beads, and a gold chalice filled with powders.

New Year's Eve. Early morning. Ray and Martha headed upstate to Albany. It was obvious that they would not be able to stay in Janet's apartment, so their first stop was an hotel, the Kenmores.

The stakes so high, for once they considered the dangers involved and took precautionary measures by checking in as Mr. and Mrs.Fernandez. In the event of the proceedings backfiring, neither Janet, nor the police, would be able to locate them. Unfortunately, they had started the correspondence from their home address, and therefore were prepared to ditch Valley Stream if anything did go wrong. But neither really believed it would.

Ray prepared for the ordeal. The transformation was about to take place.

He dressed in a dark conservative suit, and with the aid of make-up, lent by Martha, aged his features. He shaded beneath his eyes with a grey mascara, smudging it on with his finger. And then, using a brown eyebrow pencil, darkened the lines on his forehead and around his eyes. Taking up a toothbrush, he brushed up his eyebrows. A few grey strokes in his hair and toupee with the same toothbrush, and Charles Martin appeared from the bathroom.

It was the first time Martha, or anyone, had met this suave middle-aged charmer. To her, he looked: "a little too old, but good enough to eat."

Which is what Martha did when he had departed. Slipping into a black lace negligee, she settled back in the bed with a big box of candy, a **True Romance** magazine, and the thought of ten thousand dollars.

Equipped with a small bunch of red roses, and the gold bracelet given him by Martha as amulet, Ray called at Janet Fay's hotel apartment.

His intention was to make a quick reconnnaissance and report back the lay of the land to Martha before taking in the battalion.

...He enters the room, crosses to the lady in white. Old and withered, her craggy face forces a smile. He tries to strike up conversation. She smiles, but does not speak. He is lost for words, his charm falters. She motions to the far wall. It is laden with treasures. Gold and silver, rubies and diamonds. Ceiling to floor. He goes to it, stretches to it. Further and further. It recedes, refuses his touch. His wrath flares at the unobtainable riches. She takes his hand, leads him to the exit. He opens it, makes to leave. He looks back in anger at the ancient crone. Her body changes, her clothes part, her features soften. She is Jean Harlow. The platinum blonde. The bombshell. He sways to the harlot. A hand prevents him. An arm tugs him. A body blocks his way. Martha is here...

Martha awoke the instant Ray came into the room and closed the door.

"What happened?"

"First, I gotta pee." He rushed through to the bathroom. "I'm dying," and left the door ajar.

"Whadda ya holdin' it in for?"

"Where do you find a bathroom in church?"

"What were you doing in a church?"

"We went to pray together, and we lit a candle for the dear, departed Mr.Fay, whose loving spirit brought us together."

78

"She sounds senile!"

The toilet flushed and Ray came through the doorway.

"Getting near that age," he sighed. "She's at least *ten* years older than she said. Sixty-five if she's a day."

How had her dream known? thought Martha.

"She didn't think you were too *young* for her?" Martha said, amazed.

"Not at all" He sat in a chair. "I reminded her of the late and lamented Mr.Fay when they were married. She doesn't seem to realize how long ago that must have been. She says we have so much in common that a little difference of age doesn't matter." He slapped his knees and rolled his eyes. You should have seen her face when I said I also was a Catholic." He laughed. "You know who she reminds me of?"

"Who?"

"Your mother." Explaining, he added: "She's old enough to be mine."

"My mother's not Catholic." A true nonpracticing Protestant, like me.

"Well, you'd better be tomorrow when you meet Janet."

"Tomorrow?" She'd expected to meet Janet tonight.

"Yes. We're spending the day with her to celebrate the New Year."

"What about," she struggled up, "the ten thousand?"

"She's got it all right. And she can't stop talking about it." He moved to the bed as if more secrecy was needed. "She tells me everything. It's in cash and in three banks. And don't worry, I'll get it from the silly old bitch. I think I've got a way. Gotta work fast though."

"Very good," Martha beamed.

"What we gotta watch out for is the daughter and the husband."

"Yes?"

"They're gonna visit her tonight...And what would you like to do most the last evening in the old year?" Ray added, changing the note and urgency of his inquiry.

"Guess?" Martha grinned as the tension relaxed.

"I'm not too old for you?" his eyes teased as he leant over her. "A man of forty-five?"

"No, you're not."

She pulled him down on top of her pouting lips, relieved that she had rescued him from that terrible dream. One Messalina was ample.

The Victim

name	Janet Fay
color	white female
age	65
height	5' 2"
weight	143 lbs
hair	gray, tinted
eyes	brown
complexion	pale
scars & tattoos	none
others	slight hunched back

Huddled over tea round the coffee table in Janet's tiny, tiny, plain hotel room the following afternoon, were Janet, Ray and Martha, and Lucy.

The couple from New York *were* impressing Janet.

"Fifty nurses under your supervision, Martha," said Janet. "I don't know how you do it. Isn't she wonderful, Lucy? So much responsibility, and so young."

"I should say so," said Lucy, also immensely impressed. "I don't know how the hospital can do without you for a whole month, Mrs.Beck."

"Well, I just had to come up and spend some time with my successful brother. When he wrote me about that new house he was buying, I said to myself, 'I've got to go up there and talk him out of the idea.' At least if he was married....He's my older brother but he can be impractical."

Martha was laying it on thicker than the mock cream in

the cakes. The old dears were lapping it up.

Janet and Lucy were so gullible that they failed to recognize the inconsistencies in the stories related; Martha and Ray were so inebriated by their deceptions that they failed to notice them to.

"I guess that's because of your European upbringing, Charles," said Janet in her obnoxious guttural tone.

"Yes, Janet. My sister was fortunate being brought up in America. Although the separation was terrible for *us*."

"Well, I'm glad you're so...debonair -- so cute with your little accent," Janet consoled tenderly, to help him over the memory of his sad childhood.

"And even though you speak differently, I'd know you were brother and sister anywhere," said Lucy, knowingly. Wouldn't you, Janet?"

"Oh, yes. They're like two peas in a pod," Janet dismissed matter-of-factly.

Ray hadn't time to feel insulted, although the possibility did occur to him. Martha was reminded of the affront her mother had received by being compared to this odd-ball Janet. Who'd want to hump her?, she'd thought on first seeing Janet's back. A standard nurse's joke.

"Oh my goodness," exclaimed Lucy. "Is that the time? I'm having such fun with these people, I hate to go."

She lifted herself from her chair. Ray followed her lead politely; his manners were impeccable.

Janet was not so rapid in her rise. She hauled her partially deformed body up and turned to Ray with doe-like eyes. He really was every bit as wonderful as Mr.Fay.

"Can I tell her, Charles?"

Martha's stomach turned at the sight of Janet making eyes like a sixteen-year-old.

"Go ahead," said Ray.

"Charles and I are going to be married," Janet purred.

"Janet, that's wonderful. I can't believe it."

She hugged Janet lightly, so as not to ruffle their feathers.

Who would have thought it? Lucy only imagined Janet corresponded for company, to break the monotony of loneliness.

"You're the first to know, except for Martha of course," said Janet, a sick grin creeping across her face.

"Oh, it's like a dream. I can't believe it. After all these years."

"Well, it's not a dream and you're right, the three of us have a lot to discuss."

"So I'd better run along. Of course." Lucy turned to the door. Like many old women, Lucy stuck with her coat on when not in her own home -- no matter whether indoors or out, hot weather or cold. This particular day was mild and dry; unusual for the time of year. "I'll phone you later, dear."

"I won't be here," Janet said, and continued self-satisfiedly. "Tonight I'm taking Charles and Martha to dinner."

"Oh, how nice." Lucy *was* pleased.

"But call me early tomorrow before Mass, all right?"

The two hens clucked in the doorway.

Lucy turned to Martha and Ray. What a handsome catch.

"Goodbye, you two. It's been a treat meeting you. Congratulations and Happy New Year."

Neither Janet, nor Lucy, had come to terms with their age. The were too absorbed in pecking at fantasies of a life they'd missed to face reality.

These birds were sick, thought Martha. But she was amused by the tongue-in-cheek game she was playing. She only hoped the energy spent would be refunded by the dinner.

Closing the door, Janet turned to the visitors.

"Well, how did you like that hat she had on? *I* made it." Once again her noise rasped through the air.

"I know, dear," Ray congenialized, as he sat, "you wrote me all about it."

Here it comes, Ray and Martha both thought. The hat show. And our shop.

82

"Would you like to see a new one I just made for myself?"

"Oh, I'd love to," enthused Martha.

"Yes, indeed," encouraged Ray.

"All right. I'll model it for you."

Janet moved behind the closet and seconds later appeared wearing a semi-spherical creation, embodying a mass of white feathers in matching net, set off by a score of scarlet feathered antennae.

Ray stood up to accentuate his feelings.

"Oh..." ¡*Jolin*! He was lost for appreciative words, and luckily his hands also refrained from speaking.

"Oh, it's beautiful, Janet," Martha managed, to fill in the void.

"And I made it myself," repeated Janet with an idiotic grin. Her face creased like a foam-rubber ball. "Don't you think it's *cute*? I do think it's adorable."

She passed in front of Ray and perched between them on the couch.

Martha just *had* to congratulate and compliment the millinery design of the year.

"Why, Janet, with a talent like that you are missing a golden opportunity."

"Of course!" Ray was quick to pick up as arranged. "If you had a little shop in New York..."

"It would have to be an inexpensive neighborhood..."

"Where the rent would be reasonable. Like Valley Stream."

"Oh, Janet, what a business you could have for yourself."

"A business?" Janet piped in, struck by their perception of her talent.

"Why she would just rake in the money. Wouldn't she, Charles?"

"She would indeed. Of course, you would need some capital to get started."

"How much do you think she'd need, Charles?"

"Oh, I'd say about, uh, ten thousand dollars."

"Janet, if you decide to do this, don't worry about money.

83

I have a little savings at home. What better use could I put it to than to help you get started."

The repartee was completed. Their eyes passed the buck to Janet.

"Ohhh, Martha, how sweet. Oh how sweet you are, dear, but I don't need it." They're as considerate as Sara and Albert. "She doesn't know I have the money, does she, Charles?"

That capped it. She had played into their hands. They all smiled. The expressions the same; the interpretations different.

Now for dinner. Martha was starving. Details could be finalized over the meal.

The meal was consummated at Janet's regular self-service restaurant. It was something of a come-down after what they had been led to expect. More of a Barmecide's feast. Not that the quantity and quality of the food, or the conditions of the place, were all important. Ray was more intent on business. For Martha, so long as it was food, (provided it wasn't bird - - she'd had her fill of that today), it was food. Nevertheless, although they'd only been away a day and a half, she would be pleased to get back to her own house and her own home-cooked banquets.

Ray determined a schedule for Janet.

Tonight: Home to bed immediately.
Sunday: Mass, and a day of rest and prayer.
          (And a little packing if the good Lord would
          allow.)
Monday: Early morning -- Banks in Albany.
          Late morning -- Drive home.
          Afternoon -- Bank in Valley Stream.

He then determined a schedule for himself and Martha.

Tonight: Bed.
Sunday: Mass, and a day to keep Janet from the phone.
Monday: Early morning -- Banks in Albany.
Afternoon -- Home.
Dump Janet on the way.

N.B. Janet's only objection: she hated to waste the hotel money she had already paid for January.

A good part of the plans were carried through to a T, swiftly and efficiently.

Saturday: Ray and Martha accompanied Janet to her apartment and insisted that she retire to bed as soon as they had left, with the explanation that she would require all the rest she could obtain over the weekend, in readiness for the exhausting trip on Monday.

Sunday: The call to announce that Ray and Martha had arrived came earlier than Janet had expected, while she was eating her breakfast.

They settled in and briefed Janet on the call she was expecting from Lucy. She was to say nothing about leaving Albany, for it would be such a great surprise for Lucy to receive an invitation to stay at Janet's new home in Valley Stream. Likewise, she would ask Lucy to keep her prospective marriage a secret from everyone, so she could excite her other acquaintances with the news, after the ceremony. As part of the plot, Janet was to tell Lucy that she would contact her in a day or so when the preparations were finalized.

The two deceivers were relieved when the confab went off without a hitch.

The next obstacle was Mass. More by luck than judgment they succeeded in being late, and therefore found themselves in a pew at the back. Martha positioned herself on the other side of Ray in order to observe his movements and copy them. If it had not been for the worthiness of the cause, Martha would not have endured the constant changes from kneeling to standing to sitting to kneeling to...

Almost before the last prayer was prayed Martha rushed out into the rain and waited in the car. Ray did not object to being introduced to Father Nicholas, as it meant he could keep a watchful eye on Janet to ensure that she observed her promise, and did not let the cat out of the bag. There was no need for him to worry, the priest was more interested in the structure on Janet's head than in Charles Martin.

Once they were safely back at Janet's hotel, it was a relatively simple task to keep her occupied with packing, resting, eating out, and discussing their future. She had very little time to think about contacting her relatives. But when eventually she brought up the subject, Ray dissuaded her with the promise that it would be more effective and a much nicer idea to contact them from her new home. Janet placed herself entirely in Ray's hands, and seemed content to do as he instructed.

When the day had worn its path, Ray and Martha allowed Janet to go to bed, and they, themselves, retreated to their hotel and bed.

Monday: As decided, Ray drove Janet to Albany Savings Bank. She withdrew her jewelry, bonds and cash from a safety deposit box. Then he drove her to Albany Exchange Savings Bank where she drew a check. And last he drove her to the Mechanics and Farmers Savings Bank where she drew a check to the order of the First National Bank of New York.

All the time while the transactions were taking place Ray remained quietly in the background.

¡*Cagón*! The plans had been upset.

Ray was not at all happy that Janet had drawn checks instead of cash. Regretfully, he abandoned the scheme of dumping her on the road to New York. It now looked as if she would have to return with them to an unprepared house in Valley Stream, before his side of the mission could be completed. She would undoubtedly become suspicious if he pressed her to change the checks prior to their embarkation.

The business wound up, they rejoined Martha at Janet's apartment to gather her belongings.

Martha's annoyance at being lumbered with this millstone was barely concealed as they transferred the baggage to the car. Things were becoming too like her dream, the treasure trove having already slipped a little from their grasp. The only inconstant was that the prima donna was still withered and gray.

Now that Janet had dampened the procedure, Ray and Martha changed gear. It was imperative that they arrived on Long Island *after* the banks had closed. Martha happily dealt with that small problem, after which the journey was allowed to pass more slowly and smoothly.

Ray thought events were running on an even keel again.

Janet did not.

"Well, I'm afraid we're not going to make it to Valley Stream before the banks close, darling," Ray said with disappointment, to Janet at his side.

"You see," Janet reprimanded, "we shouldn't have stopped all that time for that big lunch. Wasn't necessary. Not at all." That girl eats too much.

"I told you, Janet," Martha said from the back. "I get nauseous riding on an empty stomach. Did you want me to throw up?"

"Oh, dear." Really, Martha. How distasteful.

"Besides," Martha continued cattily, "you took an awfully

long time at the banks. Woulda been much quicker if you'd taken all the money out in cash."

"And ride around with ten thousand dollars! Oh, that's cute. Really Martha, you don't have as much common sense as I thought."

"I want my two best girls to stop arguing this very minute," interrupted Ray. There was no need for this. So, they'd overlooked her craftiness. But they would outdo Janet in the end.

The referee's whistle restored silence for a few minutes.

Martha was rapidly losing patience with this senile bitch. She was driving her mad. Why couldn't it be as easy as Doris? Or even Myrtle? How did she ever manage to pick Janet? If she hadn't lied about her age, perhaps she wouldn't have done. The others were all better than this old religious crone. Fancy bringing her pictures with her. She'll probably take them to her grave. Jesus Christ, here they come again.

"Think I'll look at my beautiful pictures for a while," Janet purred, lifting them up in front of the windscreen. "You sure there's a nice place for them?"

"Oh, yes, of course. We'll hang them up this evening." They'll go well amongst the others. Wait till she sees *them*.

There would also have to be a hasty clear-up. He couldn't recall exactly what was lying around. *Something* incriminating was bound to be.

"That's the only thing in Albany I'll miss," Janet miaowed. "My lovely church. Everything I have goes to them you know."

Everything to the Sacred Heart Club, thought Martha. Raymond and Martha's Sacred Heart Club.

"There's a nice Catholic church in Valley Stream, too. I'm sure you'll like it," smiled Ray.

Saint Anthony's was akin to the church his father had graciously allowed him to attend on Sunday mornings, provided the farm duties were done first.

"I know I will. But I'll miss Saint Agnes." Now they were

88

on their way, she was becoming more certain she should have contacted everyone the more she thought about it. And they were certainly giving her plenty of time to think about it. They had hardly spoken a word since they'd left Albany. What would Mr.Fay have said, leaving secretly like that? "And of course, Albert and Sara too. Do you *really* think it was right, leaving like that without telling them a word?"

"Sure. Think of the exciting surprise it will be tomorrow when you call them and tell them," Ray slipped his hand from the wheel and made a theatrical gesture, 'I am now Mrs. Charles Martin.'"

"Mrs.Charles Martin. Martin's hat shop," Janet said avariciously, and chortled, "Isn't that *cute*?"

Martha choked on the choice chocolate she was chewing.

Eyeing her in the rearview mirror, Ray thought how her appetite had been put to good use today. Now they could glide through the new schedule he had hammered out in his mind.

The moment Janet set foot on the threshold of her new home, she was greeted by the crucifix in the hall. She was delighted. But the pleasure she received as she was shown each room crammed with religious effigies, grew to the point of distraction. The house was filled with too much goodness and love of God.

What would have been her reaction had she been allowed to step into Ray's workroom?

She was allocated a site in the living room for *her* two paintings of Christ. Ray nailed them up before supper.

After they had devoured a real meal, Martha suggested that Ray and Janet attend to their business while she cleared the dishes.

They seated themselves at the table, with Janet's purse before them.

"I suggest you deposit it in one lump sum in my bank," said Ray. "I did tell you you'd get a better interest rate here, didn't I?"

Janet nodded.

"But I think you'd better keep a thousand in cash, just in case we find a nice front. They might not take a check."

"Even with your references?"

He was prepared for any such questions.

"I don't know *everyone* in Valley Stream, darling." No one.

"All right. But the jewelry goes in the safe deposit box," Janet stipulated.

"Not until *after* the wedding. I want my bride to look her very loveliest." Ray was not to be outwitted.

Martha grinned as she stood discreetly in the doorway. Strip the old bird of everything, darling, she silently encouraged.

"Now what are you writing on those sheets of paper?" Janet asked, craning her neck in an effort to see.

"I have a marvelous idea."

Janet picked up the paper. One word was written on it.

"Surprise?"

"Just sign your name at the bottom of the page."

"And then what happens?"

"And then I take them out tonight," Ray cleared his throat, "and I mail them. One to your daughter Sara. One to Lucy, and one to Father Nicholas at Saint Agnes. They'll get them tomorrow morning. 'What's this from Janet?' they'll say. 'Surprise? What does that mean?' And they'll ring each other up on the telephone. 'Surprise? What's the surprise?' And then first thing tomorrow morning, we print up some wedding announcements. Mr. and Mrs.Charles Martin take pleasure in announcing their marriage, January fourth in Valley Stream, Long Island. Mrs. Martin is the former Janet Fay of Albany, New York. After a wedding trip to Miami, Florida, they will make their home in Valley Stream, Long Island, New York."

"A wedding trip!" Janet crooned. "To Miami, Florida?"

How had Charles known? Her dream trip there with Mr.Fay had been canceled because of his death.

"I might as well tell you now. That was my surprise for you." More of a surprise than you expect, when you find yourself stranded en route.

He couldn't contain himself; a broad grin slipped out. But it suited the occasion.

"Ohhhh, oh, Charles. How wonderful!" Janet reached over and kissed his cheek, before chuckling gleefully.

Ray collected himself enough to carry on to the culmination.

"Now sign the papers."

"Surprise. What a *cute* idea," Janet muttered. Postcards of Miami swam in front of her eyes. She signed them.

It sure was a *cute* idea. Ray had worked this trick once before to swindle a lady.

"And while you have your fountain pen in hand," he continued eagerly, "why don't you endorse the checks?"

"Endorse in the night?"

She was momentarily cautious this time. But she blinked away a fleeting image of Mr.Nixon's swindle last year, and began to sign them also. Charles was a respectable gentleman.

"I have to be out of the house very early in the morning to get the wedding announcements printed in time," Ray mumbled to prevent Janet having second thoughts. "I could stop at the bank first thing and put them in for you."

"Oh, Charles, you'd better hide them," she whispered, as if every wall had ears.

"Oh yes, I have a nice secret place in the cellar. I'll take them down there this very minute."

He waited impatiently, taking the checks from her as she signed, and waving them about to dry the ink.

"And now why don't you address the envelopes for the surprise letters, so I can mail them when I come back up?" he said as he rose from the table.

"We'll need another surprise letter for my nephew in Utica."

"Fine, do a few more. We could always use an extra one or two." Some he would post, the others he would save till he found an appropriate use for them.

Ray turned and went to Martha in the kitchen. Success, he smiled. And speaking loudly, for Janet to overhear, Ray said:

"Martha, you'd better come down the cellar with me. You can help me hide Janet's checks."

"Don't you want me to help, dear?" said Janet, as intended.

"No, darling, it's very dark down there," Ray said, urgently beckoning Martha to join him. "You might hurt yourself on the stairs. You finish addressing your letters while we do it."

Martha went down ahead. At the bottom they fell into each other's arms.

"If I didn't see it, I wouldn't believe it," said Martha.

They hadn't noticed in the excitement that the checks were incorrectly endorsed. Janet had signed the backs, but she had forgotten to make Charles the payee.

"What do you mean, you wouldn't believe it?" Ray sneered jokingly. "That's what you get for being *kind* to a woman and giving her *affection*."

He smiled as they embraced. El torero and his favored lady.

Janet was not to be omitted. She was nosy. She wanted to go down and inspect the hiding place too. She grasped the catch. It would not open.

"Charles, what's the matter?" Janet called. "I can't open the door. Are you all right down there?"

"I bolted the door from the inside," Ray whispered to Martha, before turning his voice up the stairs. "One minute, Janet. I'll be right up."

They kissed again. They had all the time in the world. Janet could go to hell.

Eventually, Ray whispered:

"I'll be right back."

He slowly walked up the stairs and turned the knob.

"The catch has slipped," he said coldly and blatantly. "We're locked in down here."

"Oh dear God. Can I open it from this side?" Janet flustered.

Janet did not relish being locked in or out from those closest to her, for when she was nine-years-old, she had locked her friend into a room for a joke. Unfortunately she hadn't realized that her friend had to be injected for diabetes every few hours. Annie had been found collapsed and ill later that day. The fright of knowing that she had nearly killed Annie had an everlasting effect on Janet. Not only did it make her paranoic about locking and bolting doors, but it also turned her into a more devout Catholic, in an effort to recompense for her stupid error.

"No, Janet, it won't open," Ray said.

"Well, goodness. Shall I get help?"

"No no. There's an outside entrance, Janet. In the backyard. But it's locked also, and it's gonna take me some time to get it open, dear. You might as well get ready for bed in the meantime." *Then I wont have to see or hear you again tonight, if I'm lucky.*

"Oh, poor Martha, she's so tired." Her immediate panic had subsided. At least they could get out. There was no danger.

"Well, she's fine." He paused, smiled. "Martha doesn't mind a bit."

The champion acknowledged his admirers and stepped down into the ring to ravish the creature.

The comforts of the bed were pleasing after the cold concrete floor of the cellar. Comfortable, but not as pleasurable -- for Ray was sleeping on the couch in the living room, while she had the fowl Janet for company in the adjacent single bed.

Martha was tired, fell straight into sleep.

Janet was not. She worried. Everything was strange to her

after her many years of full routine. The people. The house. Even this bedroom, with its abundance of religious symbols.

She had re-inspected the house while they were locked in the cellar.The only two beds in the same bedroom had puzzled her. But then she had thought, perhaps one had been moved from Ray's workroom, especially for her. She had not been able to check for she'd found the room locked.

All in all, the excitement and rapidity of action was too much for her creeping years.

She switched on the bedside lamp. That was the easiest method of waking Martha. It succeeded.

"What's the matter? Can't you sleep?"

"No. I'm terribly restless. I guess I'm not used to a strange bedroom," Janet moaned

"Do you want a sleeping pill?"

"No, no I never take pills. Not even aspirin."

"That's too bad," Martha said. Nothing would give her greater pleasure than to put Janet into the land of Nod. She turned over and tried to sleep again.

Janet was sitting up, watching. It was frightening living in a house once more. After her husband had died, she had been scared of living alone in a large house. It was such tempting bait for thieves. The hotel was much safer - only one door to bolt and bar.

"Oh, I'm keeping you up. I'm sorry," Janet recommenced, her voice grinding on. "You must be tired, locked up in the cellar over an hour."

"Janet. What's worrying you ?" Martha said turning back, curbing her impatience.

"Well, the outside cellar door. The one you and Charles got out of. Do you recall whether you locked that behind you? We have quite a bit of money here in the house to be sleeping with a door unlocked."

"All the doors are locked *tight*," Martha said, aggravated. "Now go back to sleep. You have a big day tomorrow."

"I'll try."

I hope tonight's not going to be a repeat of Myrtle, thought Martha. I don't want to hear another cluck from you, Janet.

Martha turned off the light.

Janet prayed silently .

Hail Mary full of grace the Lord is with thee blessed art thou amongst women and blessed is the fruit of thy womb Jesus, Holy Mary Mother of God pray for us sinners now and at the hour of our death amen,

and then worried some more.

"Do you think Charles is all right on that little couch down there?" Janet's voice crowed through the darkness.

That silence was short-lived.

"He's fine. Now do you have any more questions, or can I go to sleep?"

"Well, if you weren't so tired," Janet ran on, switching the light, "I would like to have a little talk with you."

"About what?"

"Well, about your brother and about you too, I suppose."

"What about us?" Martha said, and sat up.

"Well, here I am sleeping under the same roof with you and I hardly know you."

"Whadda ya want to know about us?"

"Well, I really know hardly anything about Charles. What about his past for instance?"

"Don't you think two in the morning is a little late for family histories?" bawled Martha.

"Well, here I've endorsed all my checks and I don't even know where they are," Janet squawked.

"For God's sake, Janet, *you* asked him to hide them in the cellar."

"I know, but now I don't even know where they are. Annnd you were down there such a long time."

"We were locked in!"

"I know, but right after you came up, Charles went out to mail my letters, and you and I came to bed, and nobody told me where you put them."

"Do you want me to take you down there *now*, and show them to you?"

"Yes."

Martha's voice was getting louder. It had awakened Ray. *Otra vez.* He propped himself up to listen to the raging battle in the pen above. His wandering eye caught the glint of the hammer, *el martillo*, in a stray beam of moonlight. It rested on the table below her paintings. He thought someone should brain one or other of them so he could get a decent night's sleep. Preferably Janet, as she was whining so.

"Well, I'm not going to. The door from the kitchen was *stuck*, or don't you remember?" Martha shouted.

"Well, maybe Charles isn't a sleepy head. Maybe he'll show them to me," Janet wailed.

"I wouldn't *repeat* to my brother some of the things you just said to me. I don't think he'd want to marry a woman who doesn't *trust* him. Now you get back into bed," she pointed, "and go to sleep, and I won't tell him about this conversation."

Janet pulled her legs back in, and Martha turned out the light.

Why didn't someone put this finicky fool out of her misery years ago? My, is she a broody hen. Someone should stuff her. And she's sure got a bee in her bonnet about the safety of her money.

"I can't sleep. I'm very upset."

Martha tried to hold her patience and again switched on the light.

Albert and Sara were Janet's advisors. She consulted them about every move she made. Always.

"What are you upset about *now*?"

"Well, I should have called Albert and Sara. I should have told them what I was doing. I didn't know you were going to sweep me off my feet and bring me here. They probably phoned the hotel and were told I checked out. They're probably worried to death about me right this minute."

Probably glad to see the back of you if they had any sense, thought Martha. I can see why they don't have you living with them. You jane.

"They'll get the surprise letters in the morning."

"How do you know about the surprise letters?" screeched Janet. "You weren't even in the room when we did them."

"I overheard you from the kitchen," Martha admitted coolly.

"Why were you eavesdropping on us?"

"Charles also told me whilst we were in the cellar. Okay? What's the matter with you, Janet? I wish you'd let me give you a sleeping pill. You're getting yourself all upset over nothing."

"Nope. I want to use the telephone. Where is it?"

"What do you want to use the phone for?"

"I want to speak to Albert and Sara. I want to tell them where I am."

"Well, you can't. The phone is downstairs in the living room and you're not going down to wake my brother in the middle of the night." She'd have to be firm. "You can do it in the morning."

"No, I want to do it now." Janet got out of bed and pulled her pink chenille bathrobe over her gown. "I want Sara's advice about those checks I signed over to your brother."

Martha threw back the bedclothes and jumped out. She moved quickly across to Janet.

"Now you get back into bed and we'll settle it all in the morning."

"Well, why can't I call her now?" Janet cackled.

"Because it's too late, that's why. You'll upset her."

"I said you could call her in the morning. Now *get back* into bed. I'm going to give you a few sleeping pills."

"No, no," Janet shouted, as Martha advanced with the

bottle of pills.

"Well, get back into bed!"

Janet stood stock still.

It was wicked of Martha not to let her phone. Beneath that skin she wasn't nearly as nice as Charles. She wouldn't have her here when they were married. Not even for visits. Mr.Fay wouldn't have put up with Martha like this.

Martha pushed her towards the bed.

"Don't push me like that!"

Her protest wasn't heeded. Martha pushed her again.

"Get back into bed!"

"No! You're the most brazen bitch I've ever seen!"

SLAP!!!

Martha had hit her sharply across the face. That was enough. As much as she could stomach.

Martha turned to the door and stamped out down the stairs, flying into the living room, her white nightgown sucked in among the bulges.

"For God's sake, Ray, give her back her checks, take her to the train, and send her back to Albany!"

Ray was sitting on the edge of the couch, his head in his hands, remembering the scene with Myrtle. He looked up at the two figures: the gorgonian, and the pathetic.

Janet did not understand.

"Ray, Ray? Who, who's Ray? Who's Ray?" All at once she was afraid. Who *were* these people? "I want to call my daughter and she won't let me." She fell on her knees and implored Charles. "She won't let me. Why is she calling you Ray? I'm frightened."

"She wants her checks back," Martha said.

"I heard. I heard," he said slowly and coldly.

"Oh, no. I don't want them back, Charles, I just want to call Sara. I don't want her to worry about me that's all. Can I call her please, Charles, can I call her?" She was terrified, almost hysterical.

Ray and Martha watched the mass of flesh and bone grovel

at their feet.

"I'll call and surprise her now. All right? She's worried about me. Please let me call her."

"Just let Martha give you a few pills," Ray said peacefully. "You're very upset. They'll help calm you down, and then you can call your daughter."

Her eyes told him she would not take them. He leaned forward and pushed her over. Suddenly she disgusted him. They must shut her up or they would all go mad. *Esto ya no se puede sufrir*.

"No, no please. Why do you want to give me pills? I'm afraid of pills."

"Ray, what are we gonna do with her?"

Janet scooted across the floor, away from them. She reached her trunk and rested against it.

"Ray, Ray I don't want the checks back. No, I don't want them back. IIII'm not going to call Sara, all right? All right, Ray? I just want to go for a little walk by myself and think things over." She reached in the trunk and felt around. "I just want to get a little fresh air and I'll be right back. I don't want the checks. Leave them in the cellar..."

Ray cast his eyes round the room. Quiet her. What with? His eyes again caught sight of the hammer, fixed on it. Knock her out.

"...where you hid them. Please go back to bed. I'll be right back. I'll just get my jewelry out of the trunk. Put it in my..."

Martha followed Ray's eyes and alighted on the hammer.

"...overcoat, that's all. I can't find it. It isn't here. Somebody took..."

"You've got to do it."

"...my jewelry. Where is it? I can't find it..."

"I don't want to."

"...It isn't in here. I'll just go for a walk and then..."

"If you love me you'll do it."

"...I'll be right back. I'll leave the checks here and the

jewelry. I won't take anything with me. Nothing at all. I won't even get dr

"Now!!!"

essed."

Martha brought the hammer down on Janet's head. A dull thud sounded as it sank into the skull, shattering the bone. Janet screamed. Her eyes contorted in absolute terror. She slumped forward onto the trunk, her body shuddering, straining. The tissues tried to reorganize the disarray. Bowels excreted their waste. She moaned.

"Hit her again!"

Martha again wielded the heavy hammer high above her head and swung it rapidly into the mash of hair and bone and brain tissue. Janet screamed, shaking. The crown caved, crumbled. Tugging the weapon out of the cranial gorge, she walked away from the body, the hammer swinging at her side.

"Finish her, Ray."

Ray crouched beside the dying mass. He wrung the neck as he had wrung the chickens'. The death gurgle would not stop. Blood seeped from the mouth. Spasms of life still existed. It was squirming inside, resisting all efforts to choke it.

Martha had grabbed a stocking from the line in the kitchen. She thrust it at Ray.

"Here, tie it on."

The nylon was wrapped round the neck. Ray attempted to heave out the last shreds of life. Blood clouded her ogling eyes. The lashes clotted with the balls. Blood frothed and foamed from the volcanic cavity. All form of intelligence spluttered from the gape. Every orifice issued its blood. And still it moaned.

"Get her off the rug," Martha said coolly. "She'll stain it."

Ray wrenched the nylon to drag the weight onto the carpet. It stuck. A final jerk freed it to lunge onto his chest. Boiled blood burst and broke towards his face. Pulped plasma sponged from the hollowed pate. Panic-stricken, he pushed it away. It continued to moan.

"Here. Use this as a tourniquet."

Hammer was tied to nylon. Ray started to turn." Help me," he pleaded.

Martha added her hands to the turning device. Hand over hand they turned till the body trembled and groaned no more. It lay silent and still. Stiff, and dead.

Ray rocked back on his heels and looked at Martha, who knelt and felt for the pulse and heartbeat.

"Oh God! *¡Dios me libre!*"

Ecce homo: For the first time he thought of what he'd just done. How had they managed it? He didn't know. He didn't mean to do it. He just wanted to quiet her. To shut her up. But she wouldn't stop her noise. He shivered as he sobbed at their foul deed. These hands had done it. He looked at the blood-stained limbs. His shirt. His chest.

"I'm covered. I'm soaking in it," he quaked with disgust.

"It's nothing. It's just that you're sweating. Take it off or you'll catch cold."

Martha had regained such composure as she had lost. Working in a mortuary, when first a nurse, had familiarized her with the coldness of death. To control Ray was her sole task.

"Oh, God. There's so much blood from the body," he mumbled, dabbing and wiping his chest with the unsavory shirt.

"It's all right," she comforted, and held his arm.

"The noise. Did anyone hear? God's sake we're gonna die!" His eyes flashed round the room searching for the crowds and came to rest on Martha.

"Of course not. Nobody knows what's happened." She looked deep into his eyes. "Only you and me."

They held the pose for some seconds ----- parted, as a sense of incomprehensible embarrassment dropped its barrier between them.

He stared at the human garbage. Momentarily, he felt the hatch on his head. The GORE. He rubbed the scar.

"I *need* a drink."

Whilst he went to the kitchen, Martha collected the deceased's coat and bundled it round the head. She glanced at the fanny, she glanced at the hammer...then pulled the ridden-up clothes over the thighs.

"You silly cow."

She ripped the cross from the neck and went to the bedroom to throw it with the rest.

No one *had* heard the lioness kill for her mate.

Ray returned to the scene, and taking off his soiled pajamas, dropped them onto the remains. He walked up to the bedroom.

    "Deja que te déa un abrazo."

Ray took Martha in his arms and clung desperately to her. They were locked together. Forever. He sobbed at her breast, and she mothered him. The tears that trickled to her flesh he licked away. His tongue circled the nipple and he closed his mouth on the teat. It hardened as his teeth clipped it gently. Sliding and stumbling over her skin he caressed her curves. Her breasts, her belly, her thighs, her crotch. The fat lips opened at his beck. He slipped a finger between the petals, squeezed it together, like a hamburger. The finger slithered to the tip, tickled and plunged into the blossom. He worked the juices that poured from her. Churned the fluid like a true farmer's son .

It was what she wanted, what she needed. The *coup de grâce* to an evening's work. She helped his head down to her muff. She thrilled as his tongue tickled her clit . Nothing else mattered. The idle boasts of courage and violence meant nothing to her yearning body. His passion was all it desired. It would drink no less.

He swirled his tongue through the oozing juices. Chewed and sucked the honey of love. Nipped the bud in the spring

102

field. He felt her hands pull at his legs. He let them ride, and sensed her lips. They stroked his thighs and nibbled his prick. He clenched his muscles and stiffened his length. Her mouth seized the head and sunk down hard. Up and down. Round and round. The tip. The core. The tip the core.

Venus wanted his love, his sperm, his body. She tongued the stem that throbbed in her mouth. Gobbled it greedily like a stick of candy. She caught the tang of heaven in her womb. It was ready for flight. She could tell. Off the ground. It was rising. Up to the sky. To the clouds. To the air. The air, the space, the space the stars and Goooooooood.

They drank hot and thick at the banquet of bliss.

They lay silent and still.

After a while Ray climbed the bed to lay beside his satiated goddess.

He rolled his hand through the folds of fat, played with the slabs till they slunk away. He caressed her buttocks in his palms. Felt them flop in his arms. He wedged his hands deep in the crack.

She separated their lips and rolled onto her stomach, raising her body onto all fours. She parted her legs and presented her flower for him to pluck.

He rocked back on his heels to admire. He split the bush that choked the bloom. His prick it jumped, like a cavalry horse awaiting the charge.

She reached through, grabbed his rifle, and brought it to the rim of her sopping cunt. It slowly sank into the warmth. She fluttered her bud as it struck the base. Emitted a gasp of pain and pleasure. Felt the retreat, the advance full force. She tightened her muscles, held it in place. Loosened her grip, let it slip back. Beckoned it in. Beckoned it deeper.

He pulled it out and slid it down. He rolled it round, rotating her ass. Plunged it back, right to the hilt. Pulled it out and rolled it again. Winced at her lurch back on it. He fumbled her breasts, held her thighs, controlled the thrusts.

It's coming. It's coming. She could see the ship. Deeper

my love. Deeper. Here it comes, low and fast. Hit the sea, hit the ocean. Push it from here to eternity. Faster. Faster. Do it soon. Off to the stars. My Hollywood star. Higher. Higher. Higher my love. Show the sword. Show the gold. Show. Show. Show your. Oscaaarrrrrrrrrrrrrrrrrrr.

...She awakes, turns to her side. The woman is gone from her bed. Down the stairs, into the room. She stands before him. Naked and wrinkled. Her features droop to the floor. He refuses to look, she offers and begs. She grabs his Oscar, raises it high. Raises it high. Raises it high, brings it down on her head. She cries, dies...

Next morning when they finally awoke they had breakfast as usual, before setting to work on clearing the blockage.

They lifted the corpse into the trunk -- Martha at the head, Ray at the feet -- and dragged it down to the cellar till later.

Ray was glad to see the back of it for a while. It made him feel sick.

The Venus in blue jeans went down on her hands and knees with a bottle of Clorox to scrub away the stains of congealed blood. The carpet, the wall, could be restored to their former state, but the rug had worn its years. They would have to dump it in a trash can somewhere and buy a similar one to replace it.

Every stain and smell in the house could be obliterated, but how could they remove the body? This was the main headache to be relieved.

Their plans had not accounted for *this* deed.

Idea after idea was suggested and rejected as they went about the process of cleaning. The risks and difficulties of smuggling the body out of the house, to throw it in a river or bury it in a lonely spot somewhere, were enormous. The voyeuristic community of old folk in Valley Stream would make it practically impossible.

One of the best solutions was to find a deserted cellar and

bury it there. But as they were loathe to take the body off the premises, they decided they would make a go of burying it in their own cellar.

Ray became almost enthusiastic, for he realized that he should be capable of making a good job of this task, as he could apply the knowledge he had gained from laboring on a building site.

No one would know the difference afterwards, he proclaimed.

Later that day Ray made a start and dug a hole in the cellar. When it was three feet deep, he helped Martha empty the contents of the trunk into the pit, adding the two paintings to crown the burial.

Ray stored the empty trunk in a corner of the cellar, for it surely would be useful someday if cleaned up. The only other point would be to paint out 'JF,' and paint on 'RF.' Although his baggage was initialed 'RF,' he still adopted the pseudonym, Charles Martin, without it ever coming to the attention of anyone. He tempted providence in his incompetence.

That night, Ray stole a bag of cement from a construction company and re-cemented the concrete he had broken in making the grave. After a few days nobody would know the difference. He had done a professional job. The funeral was over.

The financial side had still to be straightened out. When Ray produced the checks to pay them into his Charles Martin account, he realized that they weren't payable to him. He knew it was useless to try to cash them anywhere, but Martha maintained that she'd find a way.

She took the first endorsed check back to the bank in Albany where it had been drawn. They refused to cash it . But on dreaming up a story of how she came by it, they accepted the incorrectly signed check. With the first luckily cashed, Martha set out with the second. This one was more difficult, as it was a draft on the First National Bank of New

York. Upon her first refusal she demanded to see the manager. After a number of interviews, in which she used the same story as before, they agreed to collect the money for her.

She had succeeded in obtaining *all* Janet's money. Ray was extremely pleased. Martha had accomplished the impossible. The gods had not abandoned them.

Whilst Martha was on her travels cashing the checks, Ray sorted out any further inquiry as to Janet's whereabouts. He took the remaining sheets of paper marked 'Surprise,' and after removing the unwanted word with Clorox, he typed an explanatory letter to Albert and Sara above the signature. He recollected how, nearly two years previous, he had employed this trick to obtain his Manhattan apartment.

As he typed, he almost regretted not having planned the murder. If they had, he would have made Janet write all the letters beforehand.

Dear Sara and Albert,
  By the time you receive this letter I will be Mrs.Charles Martin on my way to Florida, where I will live with my new husband.
  I am all excited and having the time of my life. I never felt as happy before, for Charles is so good and nice to me and also his family. They have done everything to make me feel comfortable and at home.
  I will close now with my love for you both. I really do miss you all but I am sure that my prayers are granted me by sending me this wonderful man.
    God bless you all,
      Love,
            Janet J. Fay

With the ends tied up, they washed their hands. They were happy together. Like holly and ivy, they were inseparable. Murder was better than marriage. Nothing could part them now.

DELPHINE & RAINELLE

> We do not care about our reputation in towns where we are only passing through. But when we have to stay some time we do care. How much time does it take? A time proportionate to our vain and paltry existence.
>
> *Pensées* — *Pascal*

With everything in order, Ray very soon became irritable again. His need to work was compulsive. Although they now possessed the love of Anthony and Cleopatra, the daily routine remained tedious. They would have liked to move away and settle down in a more select district. Perhaps then they would get married. Not that it was necessary. They were bound together in homicide: they had Janet's ring as testimony. That and the chain from her neck were the only traces of Janet. Every other vestige of her existence was dead and buried in the grave. No address survived to pinpoint their home. There was no urgent reason for moving on yet. Only the urge to live elsewhere -- drowned by lack of funds.

Ray took out his letters from Delphine Downing, re-read them, and accessed her wealth by the application of the supreme powers bestowed on him by his apostles.

It came to pass that Delphine was a sensible woman with a fair amount of money and that security for her daughter and herself was at the heart of her life.

Despite the fact that Martha had asked Ray not to carry on with this specific correspondent, and would have preferred they didn't write *any* letters under the recent circumstances, she surrendered and read the latest dispatch.

Dear Charles,

Thank you for your thoughtful Christmas greetings.

Christmas is so busy with its hustle and bustle and the lull afterwards is such a letdown. It gives me an empty, lonely feeling.

New Year's Eve I kept the neighbor's children so they could go out and the children were sleeping peacefully when the whistles blew. The only noise was when a dog set up a noise at midnight.

I've been having trouble with my old car. Maybe I should have taken the advice and bought a new one, but I need to spend so much when it could be invested for Rainelle to use later.

I have a nice two-stall garage, but when I cleaned up the shop the tools and things filled it. But gradually I am getting everything sold.

Rainelle got a tricycle from some friends and she is sitting on it now and really making a noise. Do you like children's carols? I hope you do, for if we continue to correspond, I will mention Rainelle often.

I hope I don't break the rules of our friendship correspondence by writing you before I give you time to consider my last letter.

Sincerely,
Delphine.

Perhaps this woman would be okay. She might provide enough for Oscar and her to *buy* a real nice home. Not in Beverly Hills, but somewhere West.

Delphine appeared quite serious. The letters did not consist of amorous trifles, like most of them. She certainly didn't sound a sex-maniac. But who could tell what she would become once she'd clapped eyes on Ray. They were all the same. Every last one of them tried to jump him.

Martha looked up from the letter, her eyes asking the obvious sexual question.

"I promise," said Ray, interpreting the look. "And let's be careful, she knows our address." He smiled, before adding: "Don't worry, darling, this one *will* be the last."

Once again his eyes had seized the precious stone.

Delphine experienced a moment of panic when she first read that they would visit. But it was vanquished in the bustle of arrangements and preparations.

She had been so lonely in her heart since her husband had died a war hero. All she had left of him was his memory and his decorations. Her two-year-old child, Rainelle, needed a father. Charles sounded so charming, and since he had been employed by the British Intelligence, he seemed a most likely candidate to replace the deceased. And most important, Charles loved children.

The door of 3435 Barn Center Road, Byron Center, a suburb of Grand Rapids, Michigan, opened on January 19, 1948.

Delphine watched the two visitors -- the slim, elegantly dressed Charles Martin, and the large, jovial Nurse Martha -- walk, side by side, up her wide pathway.

"Rainelle saw you arrive," she welcomed as they neared her. "She's been waiting at the window all afternoon." She turned to the child, who was clutching her skirts and hiding behind them, and said: "Haven't you, sweetheart? Say hello to Uncle Charles and Aunt Martha, Rainelle."

The three adults laughed as the child failed to overcome her timidity.

"Hallo, Rainelle. Don't be a *shy* little girl," Ray said, bending down and stretching his hand out to her. The engaging twinkle in his expression coaxed a bashful smile from Rainelle in return.

110

"She's been dying to meet you both. Haven't you, my little lady? Each time I say, 'Uncle Charles and Aunt Martha are coming,' she becomes all excited. Well, you'd better come in. Unless you want to settle down in the porch," Delphine said, laughing.

Martha laughed heartily as she stepped in ahead of Ray. This one's going to be a bit of a frolic, she thought.

In the hallway Ray courteously introduced Martha to Delphine and Rainelle, though the latter missed the formality from her position behind her mother.

After Ray had helped Martha off with her coat, they were ushered into the living room.

"I'm so glad you could *both* come," said Delphine in her fairy-tale voice. It was obvious how she spent most of her time. "Was the trip tiring?"

"Oh no, we eased it out over the last three days," Ray replied. "We've been admiring the beautiful scenery on the way. We *needed* a break and some clean, fresh air. I'm afraid it's been rather a *strenuous* life for Martha and I recently."

"Neither of us has been to this part before, Delphine," Martha butted in, to stop Ray from being too clever.

Like a bloodhound, Martha had sniffed out the snack spread on the table in the corner the moment she'd entered. She was now eyeing it while the pleasantries continued. She *was* feeling a little peckish and hoped tea would soon be served.

"If you like, we can all go for a drive sometime," said Delphine, stopping and turning her back on the portrait of her husband that hung above the fireplace. "There are plenty of lovely spots by the lake. Rainelle would love that too, I know."

"So would we," added Martha. Pity she's not a Narcissus. We could have pushed her in after we'd got the money .

"We apologize for not arriving after lunch," said Ray, "but we just couldn't rush past the last delights."

Ray's constant little attentions towards Rainelle, as he conversed, were finally rewarded. She came into the open and

111

stood in front of her mother. Delphine rested a hand on the child's head.

Ray crouched and offered his right hand to Rainelle, glancing up at her mother.

She wasn't bad looking. She had a better kept figure than most. Her clothes fitted her properly. Her face was pleasant. Nothing unusual about her. A typical, middle-class American mother, not much character, but consistent in her ways.

Martha missed his surveying eye and her first positive chance of being jealous.

"I think she's taken to you already," Delphine directed at Ray.

"That's good," Ray said. "I've got something for her in the car. If you'll be so kind as to excuse me a minute I'll go and fetch it."

He stood as Delphine crouched down to her daughter.

It's a regular seesaw round here, Martha thought. Thank God they couldn't expect her to bob up and down.

"Did you hear that, Rainelle?" recited Delphine. "Aren't you a lucky girl? Uncle Charles has bought you a present. He'll be back in a minute."

Rainelle smiled. She loved all the attention.

"Don't get cold out there. It's a little nippy today," Delphine said automatically, as if she was speaking to a child.

"I won't," Ray said, smiling.

He turned and went out.

Why had she been so afraid when the news of their visit first arrived? He was a charming man. His appearance, his manner, everything about him was captivating. Even John wouldn't have objected. He would have wanted her to battle on. To find someone to help bring up his child properly. Charles was a true front-line man. Rainelle and she had nothing to fear from him, or his sister.

"Let's sit down," said Delphine to Martha.

As Martha sat on the couch, she cast an eye around her at

112

the comforts. The highly polished furniture, the stylish suite, the bookshelves stocked with encyclopedias and informative works. She settled back to the standard female talk, putting the money out of her head till Ray and she could size up the situation once the child was safely in bed.

"It's a very nice place you have here, Delphine. And *such* a pleasant neighborhood."

"Oh yes. The neighbors have been so kind to me since John died." Delphine played over any embarrassment she might have subjected upon Martha by instinctively launching into a fresh conversation. "Frankly, I was relieved to hear that you were coming too. I thought that Charles on his own, though it would have been *marvelous*...Oh, I didn't mean it like that."

"That's all right, Delphine. I know what you meant," Martha said and laughed.

"Sure? I meant no offense."

Martha nodded her head to allow Delphine to continue.

"All right. Well, Charles on his own might have caused a bit of a scandal with the local folks. You know what it's like in these close-knit communities?"

The error had come and gone . She'd forget it. She sincerely hoped Martha would too.

"Of course. It's the same back home in Valley Stream. All purls and no plain." Martha laughed heartily again .

Martha was going to be loads of fun, thought Delphine. She sparkled like a chunky jewel in a ring. Charles and Martha would be just marvelous for Rainelle. How lucky she had been to join that club.

"I hope you don't mind," Delphine said, more confidently, "but I told them that *you* were the nurse who delivered Rainelle. And that *Charles* was your brother. And that I'd invited the both of you here for an early holiday, away from the pressures of New York."

"No, I don't mind at all," Martha confirmed. "And I'm sure Charles won't either."

Throughpout the conversation, Rainelle had been watching Martha from the far side of her mother's armchair. She wondered where such a strange laughing creature had come from. She'd never seen someone so fat before. Only in picture books. Her eyes swiveled to the door, signaling Ray's approach.

She trotted over and waited, her hands behind her back, resting below the big pink bow of her puffy dress.

When Ray entered he gave Rainelle a beautiful blonde doll that cried when rocked. She was thrilled and even came out of her shell enough to say, "Thank you," on instruction from her mother.

Ray had also bought a present for Delphine -- a box of candy. She thanked him profusely and placed them on the sideboard, knowing that they would not be eaten in this house, but that perhaps she could give them away as a present. Although, it wasn't the sort of present she would have chosen or could be expected to choose as a gift.

Having settled her guests, Delphine announced that today was the 141st anniversary of the birth of Robert E.Lee, and that Rainelle and she were having a little celebration. Martha thought it strange that a woman, who ought to be a Yankee, was remembering the birthday of a Confederate.

Delphine noticed Martha's puzzled expression and guessed the reason. She explained that it was her policy to teach Rainelle to have no prejudices towards people who fought against you in wars, and she simply taught her American history in general. That meant the bad things as well as the good. Even though she herself was a Unionist, Robert E.Lee was a great man in American history and deserved being honored on his birthday as much by her as by the people of the Southern States.

Martha wasn't over impressed by Delphine's patriotism. However, in a way she was pleased -- surely Ray couldn't fall for such an obsessive bitch?

The lecture over, Delphine brought across the food. The

114

tea was made up of a variety of carefully prepared bits, all of which Martha tucked into hungrily but sparingly. Her appetite had been whetted, and now she eagerly awaited supper. By eight o'clock she'd discovered, to her horror, that that health food snack had been the last meal of the day.

Martha could see she would be in for a thin time for the rest of their stay.

It became apparent that day, and during the weeks that followed, that Delphine's life was centered around her daughter. Although she was forty-one and had a quiet attractiveness, she had pushed it aside in preference for the child.

Little, frizzy-haired Rainelle was treated as the budding Shirley Temple. Nothing was spared to pamper the child. She was spoilt with new dresses or toys almost every day. She was reared on the kind of loyalty that killed her father. A party celebrated the anniversaries of each American hero. Her bedtime stories were from the American Heritage series.

Ray and Martha could not help but compare Delphine's lavish treatment of Rainelle to their own meager childhoods; and consequently they regarded Rainelle with (a) jealousy, and (b) hatred.

The visitors established themselves in the spacious, middle-class home and quickly became an integral part of the household. They studied the circumstances and bided their time, camouflaging their feelings about the child and mother, and in some cases, keeping them from each other.

Ray appointed himself as Delphine's financial advisor. And more, though Martha never perceived that side. He was helping Delphine to negotiate the most profitable deals in selling her properties in Muskegon, before they departed for New York and marriage. On the way, Martha and he would dump her and the kid. It would be a richer haul than they had at first thought.

Meanwhile, Martha put her old profession into practice and

nursed Rainelle through a cold, for which she afterwards suffered the complete dislike of the child, who did not take kindly to her throat being swabbed. The child had taken to Ray instead, and almost treated him as her father.

Ray hardly had a spare moment to be alone with the wasting flower. Martha was hungry for his body. And for food. The health foods Delphine was feeding them were finally getting her down. She wanted Ray to take her to town for a day by themselves.

After a "February 12th snack party" (Martha's phrase) and a lecture on the life of Abraham Lincoln, the hero who had saved the Union, Martha tackled Ray about the problem while Rainelle was being put to bed.

Ray consented to Martha's cover plan of going out next day to buy a Valentine's present for Delphine. The woman's love of occasions would be turned to good use. They would spend a day together. They could eat and bloat out. And they could check into a motel and make love.

Martha regarded themselves in a pretty desperate position for them to have to pay for a room to have sex. But Ray appeased her with his good news.

A week or so more and the deals would be signed. They'd all leave. Dump the Downings. Keep the cash. And forget all Lonely Hearts and live happily ever after.

"I promise."

But next day the plans were to change. Delphine had problems; she was worried. She packed Ray and Rainelle off to buy a puppy. Martha was annoyed at this last minute substitute. To wreck the only plan *she* had made was unforgivable.

Delphine's courage failed her now that there were only the two of them in the house. It wasn't till a few hours later when Ray and her daughter were due to return that Delphine finally swallowed her pride and sought Martha in the bedroom.

116

Turning from the window, Martha stared at the round-faced woman.

Usually pink as the flower of her name, today Delphine's only color was on her housecoat.

"I wanted to be alone with you."

"What for?" said Martha

"I have to talk to you, Martha. It's important. I'm afraid I need your advice."

How could she tell Martha? She'd think she was a prostitute, or worse. Think she always slept with men. Martha wouldn't believe that she hadn't since John.

"What's the matter?" Martha said.

"May I be completely open and frank with you?"

"Well, of course. What is it?"

" I want to marry your brother right away . Before we go to New York."

"Why do you want to do that?" What was with all this hedging? She'd been hopping from foot to foot for the last five minutes.

"Because I'm *pregnant*, that's why."

The bastard. He's done it again. He promised. He promised.

"Martha, Charles and I really do love each other," Delphine continued. "We intended to marry almost from the start. I guess we just got carried away, that's all. But you see the thing is I don't want him to know about this until after we're married. I don't want the fact that I'm going to have his child to have anything to do with it. That's why I need your help."

She crossed to Martha, who was silently gazing out of the window into the cool, early spring.

On further thought, it came as no surprise to Martha. She'd almost expected it. But he'd been crafty to keep it well hidden for so long. Her dreams had been right though. He was a Casanova, but she wouldn't admit it, not even to herself. Her thoughts continued: Oh Ray, I'm buggered if I'll let you go.

"Well, after all you'll be my sister. I never had a sister," Delphine said uneasily, to break the silence.

Don't you sister me, you bitch.

"What do you want *me* to do, Delphine?" said Martha, glancing at the pale, morose figure.

"I want you to suggest that we get married right away. Tomorrow. On Valentine's Day."

Delphine had only once doubted their forthcoming marriage. She had walked into the bathroom and found Ray minus the toupee. It had been a nasty shock, but a few days had healed the wound she had received.

"Look, I know you're upset," Delphine went on. She had to say something. The silence was killing her. "He wanted to be so sure that you wouldn't find out that there was anything going on between us. I think you're wonderful, Martha, with your old-fashioned values. Charles does too. And he's just frightened to death that you'd find out we'd been sleeping together whenever you left the house. But we *love* each other so much that we just couldn't stop ourselves. You can understand that, can't you?"

"Yes. I understand," Martha said coldly. A tear slipped out onto her black dress.

Delphine and Ray had been like a pair of chameleons before her. Every time she had stepped out of that door, Ray had stuck it in the bitch. The bastard. She knew it would happen. She just knew it. Delphine hadn't wanted her there from the start. They must have had a grand old bash when she had trooped back to New York for a couple of days.

"Martha, why are you crying?"

This was the first time Delphine hadn't seen Martha as a bundle of fun.

"I'm crying because I feel so sorry for you," Martha snarled as she turned on her.

"Sorry for *me*? But why, why should you feel sorry for me?"

118

"I'm sorry because my brother will *never* marry you now, that's why."

"What do you mean?" asked Delphine.

"You'll find out when you tell him he *has* to marry you because he's knocked you up."

"You make it sound so *awful*."

"Well, that's the situation, isn't it?"

"Well, then you've got to help me Martha. He mustn't know."

"You want me to *lie* to my own brother? Never. You've ruined everything," tailed off Martha. Another tear dropped to her dress.

Delphine retreated to the bed and started to cry.

It was her, Martha, who should be crying like that. Not you, you two-faced bitch. Why should I keep this Charles Martin pretence up now?

"Oh, God, what am I going to do?" cried Delphine.

"You're in quite a spot, aren't you?" Martha said, breathing deeply and pulling herself together. "Besides losing Charles, you'll be pregnant without a husband. The thirteenth sure is unlucky for you."

Martha could very easily get rid of the baby for her. Seemingly with a change of heart, she sat beside Delphine and consoled the weeping reptile.

"All right. I'll help you. But you've got to do *exactly* as I tell you. Get into bed and I'll be right back."

Whilst Delphine obeyed, Martha went into the next room to fetch her purse. She took out a few pills, hesitated,

Yes

tipped

a handful into her palm with full conviction.

The decision was made.

She came back in and handed over some pills and a glass of water from the wash basin.

"Here. Take these."

"What are they?"

"Well, they're allergy pills, but if you take enough of them they will abort the baby."

"Oh, no, no I don't want to do that," Delphine squirmed. John always forbid that. We tried so hard for a boy .

"Delphine, don't be so stupid," Martha attacked. "You'll have another child after you're married. This will solve the whole problem."

"They won't make me sick, will they?"

"Would *I* give them to you if I thought they would?" she softened momentarily. Her nurse's training had taught her how to feed pills. "Now hurry up before I change my mind."

Delphine swallowed them, pulling a face like a sour puss. Martha tried to feed her more.

"Here, you have to take more. You need more for that job." If Myrtle could take more of hers, so can you of yours.

Delphine fluttered like a leaf butterfly, pushed further pills aside and jumped out of bed.

"Ohhhh, I think I have to go to the bathroom for a minute," she gulped as she hurried out.

"Swallow. Swallow them, silly," Martha shouted, thinking she was running off to be sick.

The job had to be done. Martha had to force the pills down her. She was fixed in her ways. There was no turning back. Delphine deserved it . No one was touching *her* Oscar.

The sound of a car drawing up outside made Martha spring up from the bed and rush to the window.

They were back. She had a minute's grace before they would appear in the room and terminate her proceedings.

"That's better."

Martha swerved at the voice. The job had to be done.

"Here take some more," Martha quickly said.

"I don't have to. It was a false alarm."

Fuck that, come on.

"Oh my goodness," Delphine drew out slowly . The pills were having the desired effect. "I feel so woozy. I think I'd better get into bed. Ohh, Martha, I don't feel so good."

120

She collapsed on the bed. Martha fell across the body, squeezed the cheeks, forced a handful into her mouth. But Delphine slid under and spluttered them out.

"Mommy, mommy, look at the puppy. Ahhhhhh–hhhhhhhhhhhhhhhhhhhhhhhhhhh!"

Martha leapt off the bed and swept across to Rainelle.

"Shut up!" she said and slapped the child hard around the head, knocking Rainelle back against the wall.

Casanova entered behind.

"What the *hell's* going on here?"

"Watch her, I'll be right back," said Martha nodding towards the bed.

"Rainelle!" Delphine mouthed in desperation.

Martha grabbed the child by the neck and dragged her out of the room. She was too stunned to cry.

The puppy ran loose.

She threw Rainelle into her playroom closet and locked it .

Once again Ray was confronted by panic on both sides. What the hell was she doing? He looked at Martha blazing away down the track. He stared at Delphine lying flat on her back.

Delphine had been one of the few women Ray had felt any attraction to. He just might have married her had it not been for his marriage to Martha. The only way to be free from Martha would be to kill Martha. But another murder was out of the question.

What the hell were they doing now?

The scene was blurring before her eyes. Her reactions were slowing, winding down. She could just make out Charles, and lolled towards him.

"Help me. Help me," she croaked faintly.

She was utterly helpless. Her mind screamed, but no sound left her lips.

"What *happened* to her?" Ray demanded as Martha came tearing back again. He hadn't moved an inch from where he'd stopped on first entering.

"She found out everything."

"But *how*?"

"How the hell do I know, Ray?" What a time to explain. "She was going to call the police."

La policia. Fay.

Martha wasn't lying to Ray as he'd lied to her. She really believed the story herself now. Truth and fantasy were one.

"You gave her the pills?"

He stepped back as Martha barged past.

"Yes, but I couldn't get enough down her," Martha said, scooping up the pills for a second effort.

¡*Demonio*! There was only one thing to do. It was too late now.

"Leave that. She keeps a gun in that drawer. Get it," Ray ordered.

The rolling stone was in motion.

She was paralyzed as she discerned Martha withdrawing the revolver. Why Charles? Why Martha? Why? Neither her body, her mind, nor America could do anything to prevent her fate.

Save me John! Save me, God!

It was positioned at her temple.

Rainelle! Rainelle!

Fingers tightened on the trigger.

BANG!

BANG!

The revolver lay quiet on the pillow.

Two pairs of eyes contemplated the sharpness of the kill, and then were slowly, mesmerically drawn to each other.

Snapping to, Martha tore her eyes from the magnets in his and shrouded the body in a blanket before starting to clean up the bed. She went about the work in a state of total apathy, while Ray stood at the window, shaking in the sun.

Taking the matter into her hands, Martha directed him to help carry the heap down to the cellar.

They were hardly out of the room when the puppy dashed between their feet, almost tripping Martha. She swung a foot and kicked it against the wall, cursing the yelping wretch.

In the cellar Ray set to work as with Janet.

"While I take care of her," he said, collecting the tools together, "you'd better think of a way to get rid of the kid."

"How?"

"How do I know? Take her to a children's home."

"Are you *kidding*?" said Martha. "They'd ask millions of questions and she's no baby. She'd talk, the little brat."

"Put a pillow over her face and smother her, then. I don't *care* what you do, but get *rid* of her."

He busily continued his preparations for action, humming quietly to himself. He found he could control himself with this murder. And anyway, it had not caused such a gory mess

Martha turned on the faucet and washed her hands in the tub.

A glow of an idea wormed its way into her brain.

"You might as well come upstairs," she said flatly, turning to the stairs. "There's no point in diggin' it twice."

The water remained on.

Ray relaxed out of sight in the living room, while Martha proceeded up the stairs to release the child.

The muffled crying that could be heard faintly in the background throughout the murder had sucked the child dry. On opening the door Rainelle ran straight from the closet to the bedroom, in search of her mother, in terror of the large woman.

"Where are you going? Mommy's not in there," Martha called after her.

She followed the child into the room and tried to explain:

"See, I told you she wasn't in the bed anymore."

But her words were drowned by the screams of the child as she backed away.

Martha ran across and clapped her hand over the child's

mouth. She still didn't want to alarm the kid too much. She took her by the hand and tried to drag her to the stairs.

"Come on, Rainelle. Hurry up. Mommy's down in the cellar playing with the nice little puppy Uncle Charles bought for you. You remember she said the puppy would have to stay in the cellar? Don't you want to see her? We were only playing a game to fool you."

But Rainelle was not going to be misled by the horrible woman and her niceties. She dug in her heels, toppled to the floor and started screaming again.

"Mommy! Mommy!"

Martha couldn't afford to have her cries heard. With her left hand over her mouth and the other under her stomach, she picked up the kicking child, and carried her out of the room, eyeing the puppy, who poked his head out from beneath the bed. She carried her load down the two flights to the cellar.

Knowing that the captive could not escape, and feeling tired from the journey, she put the child on its feet again. Immediately Rainelle was silent, and trotted across to her mother whom she thought was as asleep.

She rubbed the curls from her face, knelt down beside her mother, and smoothed back her white dress, out of habit. With a little hand she began to nudge her mother in an effort to wake her.

"Mommy! Mommy!"

Instinct assured her that this was her mother, though only the legs were visible, the upper part of the body being covered with the blanket.

Before Rainelle could scream again, Martha had regained enough energy to snatch up the child, in the same manner as previously .

She carried her to the sink and pushed the budding child star's head under the water.

"In you go, Miss Shirley Temple."

Martha held it there for two minutes,

squeezing the neck

124

*tightly, feeling the life being pumped from the little body as
she murdered it, yet also watching herself from a distance, in
a dreamlike incapability of halting the action ,*

till the body
ceased kicking and struggling.

Then she tossed it , with disgust, on the heap.

Slowly, wearily, Martha climbed the stairs to Ray .

"You can go down now. Everything's taken care of," she
said, her voice as cold as the concrete below.

"You go upstairs and pack while I finish up down there.
We better get out of here fast."

"Where are we going now, Ray?"

"I can arrange a meeting with a very nice woman in New
Orleans." He smiled. "We can stay there right through the
Mardi Gras. Wouldn't you like that, sweetheart?"

"Yes, darling. I'd like that," she said, wearily.

Always the same, He'll never change. Have to do another.
Need more money. How much longer will this go on? Let
him hold me just one more time.

"Hold me," she said.

He took her in his arms and kissed her passionately, as he
knew she wanted.

Must get her a new mouthwash, he thought.

"And you won't make love to her?" she asked again. But
she knew the reply .

"Do you have to ask it again? Didn't I promise? I didn't
touch Delphine, did I? After a *whole* month. I never laid a
hand on her. Don't you *trust* me?"

"Yes, I trust you, darling," she said, defeated.

"We'll spend the rest of the week in New Orleans. This
will be the *absolute* last. I promise. And then on the
spring..."

That was his final chance. He had failed. She didn't bother
to listen to any more.

"You won't need that now," she cut in -- forgetting he was
still talking -- and removed his toupee. "Besides, I never

125

liked it on you anyway."

She climbed the stairs, clutching the rag.

I promise, I promise, rang in her ears. He'd lied to her once too often. She couldn't forgive him. She loved him, but couldn't share him. They would never marry. They would never settle. This was the end.

In the bedroom the octopus slipped a tentacle under the receiver and lifted it.

"Get me the police...Hello, is this the police?...This is a neighbor of Mrs. Delphine Downing, 3435 Barn Center Road. Something's wrong over there...How do I know? I heard screams and shots, that's how I know...And now something peculiar's going on in the cellar...3425. That's right...Never mind who I am, just get over here."

The mistake didn't matter. She hung up and lay on the bed to wait.

I'll be glad to give in. I'd be mad to go on. Where could we go from here? Nowhere. Sure we could go somewhere else, but it'd only happen again. Another. They'd catch us in the end. May as well give in now. I'm not running. It isn't necessary, this killing. Neither of them were. Janet or these two. They weren't necessary. Totally unnecessary. But I just can't help it. I love him. Surely he understands. He can't do it to me. Always another one. One more to be written to. One more to visit. One more to fleece, one more to fuck, one more to kill, kill. Kill. Why couldn't we stop before? Why? Must it end like this? It was so easy at the start. Then it became so complicated. Why? Why did it have to? It could have worked. I could have worked. Even if we had killed Janet, why didn't we stop then? No one will find that grave. Clever darling. But he must go on. Add to the collection. Find a way to curb his boredom. We could have found a happy life together. One doesn't have to work to stop being bored. He wants to work. Tells me he must. Tells me he must do something in life. Why can't he just love me? If he cares enough. If he loves me enough he'll stop his work. His work was before me he says. Stop work then. Stop it. You do love me, don't you? Yes, he does. He really does love me. I want him to. His eyes say they do. His eyes always said they do. Ever since he came to Mobile. Mobile and Momma. How is Momma? Your little girl is in troubled, Momma, but she isn't worried. She loves her darling, and he loves her. His eyes say yes. His body says yes. Oh, dear Oscar. You love me, don't you? You love to swim around inside me. You feel at home there, don't you? You need me to feed you, don't you, you little rascal? Rather, you big rascal. Why don't you tell your master to stop all these games? He loves me, doesn't he? Well, tell him again. Tell him I won't desert him. Say I won't tell. He means too much to me. He shouldn't have lied though. He kept promising. Why does he always promise, then betray me? Sometimes I think he doesn't want to marry me, Oscar. Do you know that? Sometimes I think he doesn't want to settle down. That's silly, isn't it? Of course he does. But why doesn't he? Always promises. Never does it. Will he ever marry me? Will he ever settle? Well, now it's too late. We'll rot our years away in prison. But our thoughts and our love will be there. We'll remember each other every day. Now won't that be cute. He won't be able to touch any one. No women in prison. He'll think of me and yearn for me. I'm sorry, Oscar. I didn't mean to hurt you, but we can't have everything, no matter how we try. But I'll think of you, every day. We won't die. We'll live on in our minds. Never die. We've a long life ahead, although apart. That's why I couldn't face suicide, Oscar. How could I go and leave him and you to all those women? If I went, he'd have to go too. It was his fault in the first place anyway. I'm not murdering him. I'm through with murder. Never going to murder a woman or a child again. But he might. I can't let him. Must put him away from women and murder and children and sex and sex. But we'll be inseparable in our minds. Like holly and ivy. The way we're together now it's more like mustard and cress.

Everything is so dirgy. Anthony and Cleopatra, that's who we are. I'm Cleopatra and Ray is Anthony. And so are you, dear Oscar. You're Anthony, too. But she had to die. She had an asp. Where's my asp? Oh, mine's the police. They're mine. Come on, you asp. Hurry up and get here. I've never had a scrape with the law before, Oscar. Never been in trouble before. Not real trouble. How funny. Don't worry though, my last thoughts are of you, darling Oscar. I love you and I love Ray right to the end. I love you both so much. You will forgive me for what I've done, won't you? I had to do it . Don't turn your powers on me when you find out, will you? Don't kill me, Ray. Remember I love you. I always will. Always, even when they take us to prison. Where are they? Come on, please. Hurry up. Hurry up. I can't stand it much longer. Please hurry and kick down the door...

CODA

(fact)

March 1, 1949.* Martha Jule Beck and Raymond Martinez Fernandez were arrested.

The events that followed were perhaps as bizarre as the incidents that preceded their arrest, and perhaps as bizarre as their relationship.

They were interviewed together at the Kent County Jail by County Prosecutor McMahon. During the interrogation Ray spoke freely and willingly imparted a detailed account of their actions. Martha agreed and backed up his every word. On being informed that under Michigan law there was no death penalty, they submitted their words to paper without any pressure. Their statements were identical. Police inefficiency, due to their overeagerness in obtaining the statements, had not insured that the couple were kept in separate rooms.

The news hit the headlines the following day. There was an immediate public outcry for the death of the murderers.

New York Police were at the time investigating the disappearance of Janet Fay. They sent to Michigan for details of her exact whereabouts. Ray obliged. But after a full day's digging they were unable to locate the body in the cellar. Once again they contacted Grand Rapids Police. With the more accurate plan pinpointing the grave, they finally found the remains of Janet Fay.

The prisoners were then demanded by New York. Despite a Michigan law, which stated that a defendant could not be extradited to another state unless he had been acquitted or had served part of his sentence in Michigan, pressure was successfully applied by public demand and the connivance of local politicians.

On March 16, 1949, Ray and Martha were flown to New York to be executed. (The trial was regarded as a subsidiary.) The understanding agreed upon was that, if they were not sent to the electric chair, they were to be returned to Michigan.

_____

* the correct date

The newspapers continued to sensationalize the weird and unlikely relationship of a grossly fat woman and a handsome man.

At the airport Dr.Perry M.Lichtenstein, the state psychiatrist, joined their party. His job was to record the couple's conversations so as to refute (or substantiate) any later pleas of *folie à deux*.

They were kept in custody at Mineola County Jail. There they were allowed to secure counsel. Martha's family employed the services of a young Manhattan lawyer, Herbert Rosenberg. Since Ray could not afford his own counsel, he was appointed the same lawyer by the court, Herbert Rosenberg.

Their defense settled, Martha was removed to the House of Detention for Women in Manhattan's Village Square. Ray was moved to a prison in the Bronx.

In their residences they were served the charge.

```
Indictment #11422 charges that the co-
defendants, Raymond Martinez Fernandez
and Martha Jule Beck, committed murder -
1st degree, at the town of Hempstead, in
the County of Nassau, State of New York,
on or about Jan. 4, 1949, in that they
murdered one Janet J.Fay, by striking
her with a hammer and strangling her.
```

In the time before their trial they were examined by doctors and psychiatrists, and interviewed by countless officials -- all of whose evidence contradicted.

The newspapers dwelt on the grisly facts at hand, and those that were not were fabricated.

June 9, 1949. The trial began at the Supreme Court of the State of New York in Bronx County.

From beginning to end, it was destined to be a farce.

It was several days before the jurors were picked to the

satisfaction of the defense. Rosenberg was concerned with prejudices against: insanity as defense, sexual abnormalities, psychiatric reports, political convictions, promiscuity, personal appearances, and many other facts which he felt sure would be brought up during the course of the trial. Eventually, ten men and two women were selected who best fitted his demands.

The courthouse was full at the trial proper. Everyone clammered to be told the lurid details -- the press, the public, and the court.

Martha pleaded insanity; Ray accessory after the fact.

To enforce the plea of insanity the defense brought out every evil facet of their characters. Martha and Ray's relationship was unveiled as perverted. Their lives were kicked about the courtroom floor. They were painted as black as possible. Even the most scandal-mongering popular newspapers avoided publishing the explicit sexual details.

On the day Martha crossed to the witness stand, she suddenly changed direction and lunged at Ray. Before she could be stopped, she locked his face in her hands and kissed him passionately. Then she proceeded to cover his face with kisses, leaving an abundance of her red lipstick. When finally she was dragged away, quite unabashed, she cried out: "I love him, I do love him, and I always will!"

The prosecution glossed over every misdeed, finding reasons to justify or condone each, excepting the murder of Janet Fay.

Many of the true facts of the case were lost because of the situation in which Herbert Rosenberg found himself. A line of defense which mitigated one of the accused automatically injured the other. For example, when it was stated that the blow which killed Janet was inflicted by a right-handed person, this assumed that Martha was not the killer. She was left-handed. However, in the interests of his other client, this line was not pursued. At one point Martha objected to the handicap of her counsel. She was overruled.

Ray also confused the case by insisting at times that Martha was evil and deserved to die, and at other times pleading for her release because he was the sole culprit .

Forty-four days after the trial had begun, the already tiring jury was subjected to a lengthy summary of six and a half hours by Rosenberg.

July 7. 8.00p.m. The weary jurors filed out.

10.45p.m. They returned to hear a reading of Ray's confession.

2.02 a.m. The request for a recess for the night was refused. Judge Pecora ordered them not to return until a decision had been reached.

In the jury room the twelve jurors failed to agree. One persistently voted Ray for manslaughter and Martha for acquittal, but by early morning had been beaten down by exhaustion.

8.30a.m. The jury announced that it had reached a verdict.

Raymond Martinez Fernandez and Martha Jule Beck were found guilty of first-degree murder.

On August 1, in preparation for an appeal, Ray changed his plea to that of insanity. Psychiatric reports did not uphold his decision, and so he reversed it to accessory.

The case was brought before the New York Court of Appeals on July 11, 1950. This time Ray was assigned a new counsel, William Richter. Herbert Rosenberg remained with Martha. Although two of the seven judges did not agree with the previous verdict, the appeal was quashed.

Settled in the "Death House" at Sing Sing prison, Martha and Ray supplied the inmates and the public with a display of their love life, the likes of which had never before been presented by anyone awaiting execution. Ray clarified all to his captive audience in the "C.C.s" (the Condemned Cells), despite their attempts to curb him, for unlike him the other occupants' thoughts were focussed on their impending fates, not on sexual adventures.

On warm days the doors between the men's wing and the

women's wing were invariably left open, only grilles to the communicating hall separating them. Whenever possible Martha would come to the women's grille to give Ray a glimpse of her. At times when he passed into the hall, he would speak loudly to his guards, encouraging Martha to appear, blowing kisses and offering her arms in an embrace. Sometimes she used to dance, wiggling her large buttocks at him.

Martha was more fortunate in that as the only inmate in the women's wing she was allowed to wander from her cell. Her days were spent reading mystery murder books or chatting to the matrons who looked after her.

Ray wasn't so fortunate, for other than exercise periods, he was confined to his cell.

Martha was also able to receive visitors at her cell, a screen apparatus being wheeled before her door, giving her a degree of privacy with her guests. The men's wing with its abundance of occupants received no such luxury, their visitors were received in a hall, behind grilles, surrounded by other inmates and guards.

It didn't take long for Ray's boastings to bring forth retaliation among the other men. Latching on to his ploys to attract Martha's attention they found ways to make the "Mail Order Romeo" (a term they lifted from the newspapers) the butt of their cruel jokes. Returning to the cells, after daily exercises, one would jibe Ray with: "Hey Fernandez, that blimp of yours gave me a big greeting today. She wiggled at me!" Each time such a remark achieved the desired result: Ray would become furious, shake his bars, hurl abuse across at Martha or down the row at the particular prisoner. Hours later he could still be found pacing around his cell.

Evidence of the fluctuations in their prison relationship can be seen in the letters Martha and Ray exchanged.

Martha's first letter, a few days after their arrival at the "Death House," refers to their appeal against the New York verdict and their attempts for a fresh trial in Michigan.

135

"Martha is not getting on the stand again if we have a new trial. I don't want a new trial if we have to cut each other's throats. Nor do I want one if it means you will refuse to look at me, smile, or speak when possible. I can take everything except a cold shoulder from you."

By the end of the letter her mood has changed:

"I am glad you waved this a.m. Thanks, darling, from the bottom of my heart. Ray--please, Ray--accept these flowers and my love.
Your own Birdbrain.
p.s. If you don't return the flowers, I'll know you added my initials to the bow knot, joining our love together with a tie so tight that nothing can break it."

The flowers were not returned. In her next letter she referred to the birds she watched from her window:

"Maybe I can train them, darling, to fly to you with a message of love, for I never want you to forget that I love you. To me you will always be the man I love...
XXXXXXXXXX
XXXXXXXXXX
XXXXXXXXXX

(If only I could deliver them in person!)"

Within the month Martha heard a rumour that Ray was thinking of turning State's evidence. She complained to him:

"Why do they tell us things to make us hate each other? Just because I heard such stuff is no sign I believe it. No one, other than yourself, will ever make me believe that you would turn against me. Now or ever-

-if I ever find out you have turned against me, I would welcome death, for having loved and trusted you always, I would rather die than live and know that you had turned against me."

Before long she was full of regret:

"I have wanted to cut my throat ever since I said what I did."

Ray next appeared to have heard rumours that Martha was to betray him. In Martha's response she wrote:

"I would like to know what you heard I was supposed to have told Mrs.----. I swear I have not told her anything that was not brought out at the trial."

In the next letter, her belief that Ray was slipping from her grip became more apparent:

"I had a terrible dream. I dreamed that ---- called me to the gate to watch you. He wanted me to see that E. had come to see you and they had locked her in a cage with you. Your arms were about her, your lips on hers... It hurts me. I turned away and when I turned--bang-- Martha hit the floor."

Ray didn't wave to her one day. She wrote:

"I wish you'd tell me what I have done to make you act like this."

The strain never let up. Within a week she was furious that he'd said "vulgar and insulting things" about her. She accused him, in almost illegible handwriting, so incensed was she as she wrote:

"You are a double-crossing, two-timing skunk. I learn now that you have been doing quite a bit of talking to everyone. It's nice to learn what a terrible murderous person I am, while you are such a misunderstood, white-haired boy, caught in the clutches of a female vampire. It was also nice to know that all of the love letters you wrote 'from your heart' were written with a hand shaking with laughter at me for being such a gullible fool as to believe them.

Don't waste your time or energy trying to hide from view in church from now on, for I won't even look your way--the halo over your righteous head might blind me. May God have mercy on your soul.

M.J.Beck."

Within days the pendulum had swung the other way and Martha wrote Ray a long and passionate letter, begging forgiveness. This state of affairs was hardly surprising, for their hopes rose and fell with each succession of appeals.

The teasing of Ray's fellow inmates took another turn when they suggested Martha was flirting with the warders. Ray became so distraught with these rumours that he summoned his lawyer and demanded to be executed as soon as possible and thus end his "living death." The allegations that Martha had a "love nest" were dismissed by the prison authorities, though to avoid further rumours they dismissed some of the warders, transferred others, ordered that the doors between the wings should be kept closed at all times and that the gates to each wing were kept locked at night to make it impossible for any male guard to cross to the women's wing. On top of this Ray was removed from the scene to the other male wing where he was the sole occupant.

This new isolation depressed Ray further. One time a hangman's noose, fashioned from a shirt, was found in his

138

cell. Greater alarm was caused though when some copper wire was discovered in his cell. It was also noticed that the cover to a lightswitch just outside his cell had been interferred with. It was assumed that Ray was trying to short-circuit the State's eventual task. From that day forth a guard was stationed outside his cell day and night.

On January 2, 1951, the Supreme Court turned down their last appeal. Only the Governor of New York could grant them a reprieve. In the meantime, the Court of Appeals at Albany set a new date for the execution. With six weeks to live, Ray was transferred back to his old cell in order to lessen his anxieties.

Both Ray and Martha became resigned to their fates. Martha, who had been dieting, lost the will to continue, rapidly regained the lost pounds.

In spite of the grislier aspects of the case, Ray and Martha received many letters of admiration. A substantial number were from lonely hearts, male and female alike. But Martha's most treasured letter arrived as she awaited her execution. Ray wrote:

"I would like to shout my love for you to the world."

Martha's final statement attacked the world that had judged her so cruelly.

"What does it matter who is to blame? My story is a love story, but only those tortured with love can understand what I mean. I was pictured as a fat unfeeling woman. True, I am fat, that I cannot deny, but if that is a crime, how many of my sex are guilty? I am not unfeeling, stupid, or moronic. The prison and the death house have only strengthened my feeling for Raymond, and in the history of the world how many crimes have been attributed to love? My last words are and my last thoughts will be: He who is without sin cast the first stone?"

To the chaplain she said:

"I know my sin was great, but the penalty is great, too. That makes things even, I guess. I don't think I need to fear what lies ahead."

Ray's last words were more resigned.

"I am going to die. That is all right. As you know, that's something I've been prepared for since 1949. So tonight I'll die like a man."

It was doubtful whether they would have escaped this fate even if they had been found not guilty or jailed in New York. There were other charges to be faced. For by now, all their murders were known, the police having followed up the list of seventeen women's names, all members of Lonely Heart's clubs, which were found in Ray's pocket when arrested. They would have had to stand trial for the murders of Delphine and Rainelle Downing in Michigan. Or for the murder of Myrtle Young in Arkansas. (Until Ray and Martha's confessions that they had robbed her, the police had believed her death to be accidental.) Or for the murder of a certain Mrs.Thompson of Manhattan whom Ray had left in Spain.

John King and Richard Powers, both twenty-two-years-old, were also to be executed alongside Martha and Ray. This caused even more jibing between the two young men and Ray. They constantly reminded Ray of their date together, adding: "Don't forget to bring Martha." Ray would snap back: "You dirty punks! I'll still be around when you're both dead." This was to be true, even if only for a few minutes, for the order of execution was drawn up according to those who had the most nerve. Ray knew the boys would break down before him and thus precede him to the chair.

Early on March 8, 1951, Ray and the two men were led from their cells and taken to the "Dance Hall," the antechamber to the execution chamber. This isolated block of eight cells was occupied on the last day by those awaiting execution in case they should go to pieces and disturb the other prisoners. As each departed they were allowed to shake hands with the remaining inmates. Ray, as much as the other two, choked into tears before reaching the end of the line. He had promised to say good-bye to Martha, but couldn't find the courage. His last chance was missed. Martha would not join the men in the "Dance Hall"; women remained in their own wing until the last minutes.

Once in their new home, albeit temporarily, a truce was called. The three men reminisced on happier times. During the afternoon the two young men were taken out to say their good-byes to their mothers and sisters.

The last meals were mainly untouched by the three men. The remains, whole courses, were delivered to the other inmates in the "C.C.s" along with a handful of Havana cigars. Martha ate fried chicken, fried potatoes and salad.

A large flock of reporters turned up to see the four executions on the night of March 8. King and Powers were the first to go to the chair. Ray followed, and Martha was last as it was generally thought she would be unlikely to break.

At 11.12p.m. Ray entered the green-painted chamber in the company of a Catholic priest. As he sat he pulled up the creases of his trousers, as was his habit. The press misinterpreted the gesture as one of defiance.

The switch was thrown. His end was swift.

At 11.24pm. Martha traced her lover's steps into the room, accompanied by a Protestant chaplain. She had some difficulty in forcing her body into the chair. A nervous twitch in her lip made her appear to leer at her onlookers.

Four shocks were needed to still her body.

APPENDIX

The basic facts behind the story you have just read are true, although a substantial amount of what are presumed to be the real facts, differ both from the film and the novel.

The film was drawn from trial records and newspaper reports, all of which contained a welter of untruths and trivial details. But in order to represent reality as simply and clearly as possible in 106 minutes, the film eliminated that which it regarded as minor. For example: no mention was made of Ray's use of Voodoo, or the facts behind the scar on his forehead.

That the time limit was compressed by five months is irrelevant to the events; but it is important to realize that places, names, and the characters of the victims had to be changed if the film was to be made. Under pressure of libel, certain facts had to be obscured or obliterated: a major example being that Martha's former marriage was ignored, and that her two children, constantly at her heels, were portrayed by the character of Momma.

Ray claimed that he had seduced more than a hundred women, but only where bigamous marriage or death occurred are we able to cull further information on which to build the story. If he had seduced many other women, only a handful came forward at the police investigation, and their names have been withheld. It is obvious why the others didn't reveal themselves, for Ray had stated that he had sexual intercourse with many ordinary, decent, middle-class females on the first night of meeting. These women had no desire to be shown up as idiots, or worse. Each one had a certain willingness to be led to her fate. In their refusal to come to terms with their unattractiveness and their sexual dwindlings, they seemed to be content to be sucked into the net. Ray's earlier victims who lost money decided to forget it and pretend it never happened. Everything they had not wanted to happen they ignored. Even during the time from the arrest to the chair, both Ray and Martha received a heavy fan mail from lonely males and females, some offering themselves in marriage, and others offering just plain sexual intercourse.

The film also differs from the novel. I have attempted to re-instate some of the points necessary to substantiate character -- particularly of Ray and Martha -- as there were sources for obtaining this information. But to remain close to the film I have omitted some of the true details, and intend to enlarge on those facts in this appendix.

I have also changed a few scenes from the film which I found difficult to believe could have happened in the way depicted. For example: after Delphine Downing's murder, Martha would have found it impossible to lead the child -- whom she had fifteen minutes earlier slapped and locked in a closet, and who incidentally already fought shy of her -- calmly from the closet to the cellar, as was shown in the film. I feel sure that no child would trust such a person under the circumstances.

Although the film was commendable in most respects, and I am fully aware that the writer took over direction (his first film) from Martin Scorcese at very short notice, he nevertheless made a number of errors and contradictions -- some so small as to be irritating rather than important. However, the Rainelle episode above, and the calm with which the police rang the doorbell at the end (after being notified of possible murder) seem unbelievable. It also seems unlikely, though I must admit that it is just possible, that Janet Fay might have been able to overlook the contradictions in the stories of her visitors. But left alone to her thoughts whilst Martha and Ray were in the cellar, she would surely have questioned the sight of twin beds in the same bedroom, considering she believed Ray and Martha to be brother and sister.

In some respects the novel intends to be nearer reality than the film; but for the same reasons as the film, a few of the facts have been altered.

From the mass of information available (the court records are 45,000 pages long), the true facts still cannot be discerned, for everyone, including Ray and Martha, contradicted. One of the only things we can be certain of is that they were guilty of murder and would have met some fitting fate as punishment, sooner or later.

Some of the truth has never emerged and never will be known. Therefore both the film and the novel have taken the liberty of fictionalizing probable scenes. We trust these are just as likely to have taken place as anything recorded.

My ideas of the victims' characters and backgrounds are entirely fictional, as there is no information upon which to draw. No offense was intended if they were made to be more obnoxious or stupid than some of them really were. It is unfortunate that real characters often cannot be used to make a film or novel a replica of the actual events when a documentary approach is proposed.

The facts in the coda refrain from comment, as here I do not wish to condone the methods by which the two killers were brought to justice. But it must be borne in mind that those methods were crucial as regards the information Ray and Martha imparted truthfully and that which they withheld or lied about. This is the sole source of knowledge we have upon which to base our work.

The factual details set out in the novel can be regarded as true, except where explained in the following notes.

The two most important factors that the film ignored were: Ray's belief in Voodoo, and his accident.

During the trial Ray was accused of "feigning religiosity" for purposes of deception. But had they consented to recognize his keen interest in Voodoo, they would have been able to account for all the religious symbols found in his home. Many practitioners of Voodoo in civilised countries have to adapt the religious objects at hand for their needs.

Court psychiatrists also dismissed the idea that Ray's accident had any bearing on his behavior; it was merely an attempt on his part to excuse his acts. But his relatives and close friends maintained that a change of personality did occur, and that he seemed to have been deprived of the ability to distinguish between right and wrong. He had possessed a normal attraction to women beforehand, having had a few affairs in Spain. And it was known that he contracted syphilis at this time, never being fully cured. But after the accident Ray boasted of the hundreds of women he'd seduced to satisfy his enormous sexual appetite.

Even as I write this, in today's newspaper there is a report of a twenty-nine-year-old woman in San Francisco who, up until a cable car crash, was deeply religious. But since she received the injury to her forehead in the accident, she has craved for sexual relations, and claims that in the last year alone had had intercourse with more than one hundred men.

It seems odd that those women he had known since his accident who could be traced were for the most part unattractive and somewhat older than Ray himself. This strengthens the probability that Ray was attracted to Martha despite her obesity. At the start of his acquaintance with Martha, Ray frequented Sammie's Bowery Follies and was photographed a number of times in the company of the large ageing women who performed there.

Martha suffered from a pituitary-ovarian deficiency which was the cause of her fatness. Although her size was tolerated by most adults, she had indeed found it difficult to obtain employment. However, she had been accepted at a hospital for crippled children in her home town of Pensacola, without question, and had been promoted to Superintendent of the Home.

146

Earlier, when working in California, Martha became pregnant. She pressed the father, a bus driver, for marriage, but he presumably preferred to attempt suicide rather than marry her. Disheartened, she returned to Pensacola to give birth to her child. It was then that she concocted the story of Joe. While still at home she met Alfred Beck, whom she forced into marriage, having a second child by him. Martha soon divorced Alfred for his adultery and received a substantial alimony.

It was her little boy and girl that Raymond first met when he visited Martha, for her mother was not living there at the time.

He had picked Martha on the curiosity value of her maiden name, Seabrook, which for some strange reason she had inserted between Martha and Beck when signing her introductory letter. He regarded Seabrook as an omen of good fortune, since it was also the name of the author of **The Magic Island**, his gospel on Voodoo.

The letter from the Friendship Club (Mother Dinene's Friendly Club for Lonely Hearts) which had arrived anonymously at Martha's apartment in November 1947 had been sent as a joke, and it was only out of defiance, in an effort to reverse this joke, that Martha answered. Immediately after Christmas she met Ray, and the latent evil that both must have possessed was released.

When Ray wrote saying that he couldn't see her again, Martha took the two children to the neighbor who usually looked after them, and returned to her own apartment to gas herself. Before the fumes filled the room, she began a letter to Ray. But her nosy neighbor, Molly A. (Bunny), is supposed to have interrupted the attempt with the help of the police. After Martha's recovery either she or Molly posted the letter off to Ray. Consequently he invited her to New York. Leaving the children with the neighbor, Martha set off for the bus depot.

On her return she was dismissed from the hospital without

explanation, and so pleaded her case in the local paper. The publicity turned sour on her. She was unable to find another job. Instead she took herself, and the children, off to Ray's place on 139th Street, New York.

He was none too pleased at Martha's unheralded arrival with the two children and insisted that she get rid of them. After much protest and weeping, Martha offered them to the New York City Department of Welfare. They asked for too much money, and so she deserted them at the Salvation Army, phoning back that she was about to commit suicide. Later the children were shipped to Martha's mother in Florida.

It is interesting to note that someone who had two children, and who wept at having to leave them, could later kill a child intentionally. Indeed, from the "Death House" Martha wrote to a Dr.Richard Hoffman: "Will you be so kind as to write to my mother and advise her how and what to tell my children about me? My daughter will be six in Sept., and will also start school the same month. You know, Dr.H., she already has two strikes against her and if I go to the chair it will be strike three. I feel that you are in a position to know how to tell her so that her little mind can grasp the truth and not be warped by all of the malicious jeers and gossip that she will have to face in the future... Martha Beck -- 108594."

DORIS:

Ray married Miss Esther H. (Doris) on February 28, 1948, at the County Court in Fairfax, Virginia. She stayed a month with Ray and Martha, but left upon hearing gossip about him, and because he persisted in his efforts to have her sign over her insurance and pension. Later, through lawyers, she managed to retrieve her car which had been taken from her and three hundred of the five hundred dollars which it was claimed by Ray she lost at a strip-poker game. But she was unable to recover her rings, as Martha had sold them.

It is a known fact that Ray was attracted to women with exotic names. Martha was a rare case, but then her attraction lay in Seabrook. Why he preferred unusual names is not known. Perhaps he wanted to retain some memory of the flowery Spanish appellations. His Spanish wife was called Encarnacion. Of the other known victims, Irene D. (Evelyn) and Janet Fay are the only two of his choice with names that were less than uncommon.

It is also of interest that he met Esther in a Spanish club while she was on holiday in New York, and not through a Lonely Heart club.

Even in New York today many single people haunt "lonesome bars" for the express purpose of picking up a mate.

MYRTLE:

Myrtle was in fact two people whom the film had rolled into one.

The first, Myrtle M., had become pregnant as the result of an earlier escapade with Ray and was attempting to force him into marriage. He quickly sold the lease of the apartment and fled with Martha to the company of Myrtle Young in Greene Forrest, Arkansas. He married Myrtle on August 14 in Cook County, Illinois. For three days the trio lived in a Chicago boarding house. The toupee that Myrtle is supposed to have given Ray had been bought long before he had even met Martha.

When Myrtle's annoyance at this strange honeymoon became too evident, she was given some barbiturates. A day later, regaining consciousness, she was guided onto a bus bound for Little Rock.

She died later in hospital. Foul play was ruled out as she suffered from a liver inflammation which was presumed to be the cause of death.

On their way back to New York, Ray and Martha visited several other club members, but their gains were small.

EVELYN:

Having rented an apartment in Queens, they set off to Irene D. in New England. During their stay Martha had persistent arguments with Ray over the seriousness of his marriage to Irene. She finally consented to leave and visit friends. Martha must have liked Irene for she had warned her earlier of Ray's usual intentions. Irene had not been impressed with the brother-sister relationship and shortly afterwards ordered Ray to leave also.

A broken man, Ray begged Martha to return to him. She did.

In an effort to stress the fact that Martha had made a genuine attempt at suicide during her life, the film inserted the imaginary drowning in this episode.

JANET:

Janet Fay replied at once to the letter from Charles Martin. Although she belonged to several clubs, she was exceptionally struck by Charles.

Before they left for Albany, Ray and Martha rented a new apartment at 15 Adeline Street, Valley Stream, Long Island, using the names Mr. and Mrs. Charles Martin.

After Ray had visited Janet briefly, Martha and he spent all their money celebrating the New Year. Next day they saw Janet together. Ray explained that his money had been stolen and that they hadn't enough to stay at their hotel. Janet welcomed them into her single room with open arms. There they remained for the next couple of days.

With all the money arrangements made -- $3500 in cheques and $2500 in cash -- they departed with a few of Janet's belongings for Valley Stream and marriage.

It is surprising that Janet so readily left her home, apparently without qualms about contacting friends or relatives.

How Janet Fay's murder came about is unknown. Martha

contended that she had blacked out, and came round to find herself holding a hammer, and Janet dead. Even when presented with the cause of death as fracture of the skull, and strangulation, she maintained that Ray used the tourniquet solely as a means of stemming the flow of blood. At a later date she said that Ray had done the murder by himself and that she had only entered to see Janet being strangled. Ray claimed that he was out of the room at the time and that his only crime was in keeping the murder a secret. He thought Martha had done it in some kind of blackout, for she had complained of such experiences before. (While in California, Martha had collapsed in the street and suffered amnesia for three days.)

Their contradictions about the murder made it impossible to ascertain what really happened. There is a strong possibility though that it took place as the film and the novel have depicted.

Who was actually responsible will never be known. There is question as to whether the blow was struck with the right or the left hand. As Martha was left-handed, it would appear that she was not the guilty party. But although Ray was right-handed he stated that he was incapable of acute violence, having been made a coward by his accident. Since both were able to supply fairly acceptable reasons for their innocence, the following question could be asked. Although it is only a very remote and unlikely possibility, could there have been a third person present?

There was in any case, no reason for the hammer to be in the room. Janet's paintings were not nailed to the wall, but taped.

Whatever happened, nobody seems to have heard or reported the killing, even though there must have been screams from the dying woman which would surely have resounded through the whole building.

To prevent the blood dripping through to the apartment below, they cleaned up almost immediately.

Next day Ray bought a trunk in which to store the body. With Janet's body safely locked inside, they took it to Ray's sister in Astoria and left it in her cellar. Surprisingly, no smell was detected before Ray returned to remove it to the cellar of a house which he had specially rented on 149th Street, South Ozone Park, Queens. Martha and Ray installed themselves for a few days only. Time for Ray to bury the body and re-cement the cellar floor. After four days of sitting around, waiting for the cement to dry, they returned to the agent with the news that the house was unsuitable.

To clear up the final details, they returned to Albany, collected the rest of Janet's belongings and stored them in his sister's cellar.

Ray's letter to Janet's stepdaughter, Mrs.Mary S. (both Lucy and Sara were evolved from this one person), was written to curb any inquiry. However, it did not -- the typed letter only caused suspicion.

With everything watertight, Ray and Martha abandoned Valley Stream and set off for Grand Rapids, and Delphine.

DELPHINE & RAINELLE:

The woman with whom Ray had been corresponding through a box number was soon seduced. Although Martha was angry when she found out, she held her jealousy, till at last she was provoked to take action upon Delphine's announcement of her pregnancy.

Who actually pulled the trigger of the gun is questionable. Martha admitted administering pills, but claimed that the dose was not lethal. At one time, Ray contended that he thought the woman was dying, and therefore he was only committing euthanasia in shooting her.

After Delphine Downing was buried in the cellar like Janet, Martha told Ray to make a run for it -- she would take all the blame. He dismissed the idea. That evening they visited neighbors to inform them that Delphine had gone away, leaving the child in their care.

Rainelle was puzzled at her mother's disappearance and rejected the friendly advances. They considered taking her back to New York, but they dared not risk upsetting her. To appease Rainelle they bought a dog next day. It was subsequently returned to the farm where it was purchased as it was far too big and rough for such a small child. A day later, they took the car to a garage for some repairs in readiness for the long journey. Once again another night would have to be spent at the Downing home because a trailer licence had yet to be acquired.

The child was creating problems. Ray ordered Martha to dispose of her in any way possible. Martha drowned Rainelle. Ray buried her.

By now the neighbors had become suspicious. Two of them called at the house on false pretexts to find out what was going on. Ray and Martha thought they had ably disposed of the pair.

Instead of fleeing at once, they decided to take in a movie. Not long after their return, two policemen arrived at the door. They were arrested after the house had been searched and the fresh cement found.

Why didn't Ray and Martha leave while they had the chance?

MRS.THOMPSON:

After the news had traveled the world, Ray became suspect for the death of Mrs.Jane Thompson in La Linea, Spain. She had died of poisoning at the end of a holiday there with Ray. The cause of death was recorded as a heart attack, but later the police thought that she might have died from an overdose of her medicine -- digitalis. Although on digging up the body they found that decomposition was too far advanced to reveal the truth, they nevertheless were willing to try Ray for the murder had he been available.

Ray protested that he had not given Jane an overdose, for she had complained of the way he measured out her medicine, and had insisted on doing it herself. Right to the end he remained bitter towards the memory of the woman. Besides the apartment he had swindled from her mother, she had never given him any money or sexual contact.

The climax of his strange relationship with this woman had been a holiday in Spain in October 1947. Ray had introduced her to his Spanish wife, and the three of them had spent a week together. What happened is not known. Presumably a bitter argument ensued. Mrs.Thompson died shortly after.

On his return to New York Ray produced a fake will laying claim to the apartment. He was living there with Jane's mother, both when Martha first arrived, and when she settled permanently. Within days the pair had plotted the dispatch of the old woman to her son's home.

Our knowledge of Martha's childhood, and her life up to the time she became a nurse, springs almost entirely from her own statements. Much is disputed. Various sources claimed that Martha was not as fat, and consequently not as scorned and ridiculed, in her early years as she insisted. Perhaps some of the facts were concocted by Martha to gain sympathy in court.

Her genuine confusion concerning truth and fantasy make many of Martha's statements doubtful. However, she was the youngest of five children with an age gap of twenty years, and therefore may well have found herself rather cut off from other members of the family.

One source alleges that at thirteen Martha was raped a number of times by her brother, but others have refuted this as a definite trial hoax.

From the evidence given, it does seem that Mrs.Seabrook (Mrs.Beck) was protective and somewhat stifling as far as Martha was concerned. She constantly arrived to spend time with her daughter, even after Martha was well established in her profession and capable of looking after herself.

Ray's background is more straightforward. I have presented most of the facts within the novel. Although the information stems from his own statements, relatives (especially his sister from Astoria) confirmed the details. The only question mark to his life story concerns his accident. Psychiatrists, who examined him while under arrest rejected its significance and claimed that he was quite sane. However, since he had not received proper treatment in the West Indies at the time of the accident, no one could be certain of his mental health.

Had Martha not appeared on Ray's horizon, or vice versa, it is quite probable that Ray would not have murdered violently (although poison may have been within his scope); Martha would not have committed any crime. The impression gained was that Ray was quite happy in his profession of fleecing. It was only when Martha joined him that some incomprehensible event occurred.

Both were completely bewildered by their evil deeds and could offer no explanation for them.

Those that suggested the murders had been planned credited Ray and Martha with little intelligence. If the killings had been premeditated they would surely not have made the many little mistakes with only futile attempts to cover up. It could have only been a matter of time before they were caught. In fact it is surprising that the police did not catch up with them earlier.

There is little doubt that Martha provided the aggressive force in the relationship, for, although Ray made idle boasts of courage, he had shied away from violence since the accident.

Why was nothing done earlier to help this man as soon as it was realized that his attitudes to violence and women had changed so drastically? And why was a lobotomy never performed on his injured brain?

Martha killed because of jealousy, which built up inside her until it boiled over in a senseless act of violence. Martha's love for Ray was too obsessive to stand by and watch when it was threatened.

Ray's eyes held some strange fascination for her. Many times she professed to be afraid of his power, afraid that he would kill her if she stepped out of line.

That her love for him was deep and true and overruled her senses is the only undisputed fact in the case.

But was his love for her real?

Right up till his last note to Martha while in the "Death House," one could question whether he was merely being kind to a companion who had irrevocably forced her life upon him. Ray must have felt a deep need of Martha, for why else would he have begged her to return after the Irene affair?

At times while in prison, Ray said that he respected Martha but didn't know whether he loved her. He seemed to be afraid of her and felt some duty to stick by her as one event followed another, and the knot of their involvement was drawn tighter.

It was doubtful that he would ever have married Martha, if only for the simple reason that, while his Spanish wife remained, any other marriage would be void. However, since marriage was the case when he didn't care for the woman, it was logical that to remain faithful to Martha without the legal ties of marriage would be a greater expression of his feeling for her. Martha was content to stay as his mistress for Ray treated her with more respect than he gave any of his wives, though she might have preferred marriage had it been possible.

Despite fairly attractive features, Martha could never have appeared less than ugly. The styles of fashion in the late forties could only have emphasized her fatness. The newspapers at the time attributed Martha's preference for black clothes to a grisly sense of doom on her part. It is far more likely that she wore the most receding of all the colors in an effort to appear a little slimmer. She had apparently come to terms with her size as she grew older, enveloping herself in a protective dream world where everything was

156

perfect for her.

The court, however, refused to acknowledge that Martha's life was a complete fusion of truth and fantasy. In doing so, they rejected the ability to understand the large woman, or comprehend her actions.

Many women must live in the fantasies of romance stories, as even now not only are such magazines and books selling well, but there's a flood of similar daily soap operas on television around the world.

But when this fantasy is upheld to the complete fabrication of Lieutenant Commander Joseph Edward Carmen of the United States Navy -- of whose existence Martha managed to convince not only friends but also business acquaintances; and of the fabrication of the character called Oscar, whom letters were found written to, and who in fact Martha proudly admitted to be her name for Ray's penis -- surely one cannot pretend that such a woman is legally sane and responsible for her actions?

The blatancy with which Martha spoke about Oscar and her sex life with Ray shocked many at that time. What were then termed sexual perversions and abnormalities would nowadays be considered normal, particularly among the young and the enlightened. For the celebration of this freshly gained freedom, one has only to look to movies, television or advertisements to be confronted with such acts.

Their inexplicable relationship, which has at times been branded as a love story, a murderous allegiance, a *folie à deux*, owes a lot more to carnality than any of these terms can credit.

b l u e   m u r d e r